Anger pierced him, sharp and sudden

He'd almost been taken in by her little-girl-lost routine. Him and the rest of the male population, apparently, Olivier thought acidly.

He'd started the evening with one aim in mind, he reminded himself bitterly. To seduce Bella. That was what he'd set out to do, and he'd almost allowed some ridiculous, uncharacteristic and completely misplaced sense of chivalry and sentimentality to stand in his way.

He should be grateful that he'd realized how foolish he was being before it was too late. Bella Lawrence wasn't the innocent she pretended to be.

She was as clever as she was beautiful, and she had played him like a fool.

As he approached she looked up at him, and he saw nameless emotion blazing in her midnight eyes.

"Are you ready to go?" he asked with savage courtesy.

"Yes, please." She came toward him without hesitation. Her lips were still swollen from his own kisses. He summoned a glacial smile. At least he could now enjoy what was on offer without guilt.

Dear Reader,

Harlequin Presents® is all about passion, power, seduction, oodles of wealth and abundant glamour. This is the series of the rich and the superrich. Private jets, luxury cars and international settings that range from the wildly exotic to the bright lights of the big city! We want to whisk you away to the far corners of the globe and allow you to escape and indulge in a unique world of unforgettable men and passionate romances. There is only one Harlequin Presents®, available all month long. And we promise you the world....

As if this weren't enough, there's more! More of what you love.... Two weeks after the Presents® titles hit the shelves, four Presents® EXTRA titles join them! Presents® EXTRA is selected especially for you—your favorite authors and much-loved themes have been handpicked to create exclusive collections for your reading pleasure. Now there's another excuse to indulge! Midmonth, there's always a new collection to treasure—you won't want to miss out.

Harlequin Presents®—still the original and the best!

Best wishes,

The Editors

India Grey

TAKEN FOR REVENGE, BEDDED FOR PLEASURE

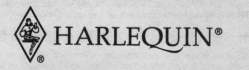

HARLEQUIN®

TORONTO • NEW YORK • LONDON
AMSTERDAM • PARIS • SYDNEY • HAMBURG
STOCKHOLM • ATHENS • TOKYO • MILAN • MADRID
PRAGUE • WARSAW • BUDAPEST • AUCKLAND

Recycling programs
for this product may
not exist in your area.

ISBN-13: 978-0-373-12824-2
ISBN-10:   0-373-12824-X

TAKEN FOR REVENGE, BEDDED FOR PLEASURE

First North American Publication 2009.

Printed in U.S.A.

All about the author...
India Grey

A self-confessed romance junkie, **INDIA GREY** was just thirteen years old when she first sent off for Harlequin's writers' guidelines. She can still recall the thrill of getting the large brown envelope with its distinctive logo through the letter box, and subsequently whiled away many a dull school day staring out the window and dreaming of the perfect hero. She kept these guidelines with her for the next ten years, tucking them carefully inside the cover of each new diary in January, and beginning every list of New Year's resolutions with the words *Start Novel.* In the meantime, she gained a degree in English literature and language from Manchester University, and in a stroke of genius on the part of the gods of romance, met her gorgeous future husband on the very last night of their three years there.

The past fifteen years have been spent blissfully buried in domesticity, and heaps of pink washing generated by three small daughters, but she has never really stopped daydreaming about romance. She's just profoundly grateful to have finally got an excuse to do it legitimately!

This one's for Daisy, who makes the hard times easier and the good times better.
With love and thanks.

CHAPTER ONE

WAVES lapping on a silver-sanded beach... A warm breeze sighing through palm trees... Or how about, a wide blue sky filled with marshmallow puffs of pure white cloud...?

Nope. No good.

Bella Lawrence's eyes snapped open and she bit her lip, focusing hard on the dainty French wirework chandelier currently under the auctioneer's hammer. There was absolutely no point in trying to think calm thoughts at the moment; not while her heart was beating at roughly twice its normal speed and her hands were slick with sweat.

Not while she could still feel his eyes on her.

She wasn't sure when he'd come in, only that he hadn't been there when she'd taken her place at the start of the auction. She'd felt a growing awareness of heat on her skin and a tingling sensation in the pit of her stomach, and when she'd turned her head he'd been there. Looking.

At her.

Maybe she had lipstick on her teeth...

Sweeping her tongue nervously across them, she allowed herself another very swift glance from under her eyelashes, and felt her stampeding pulse rocket again. He was standing by the wall, making no attempt whatsoever to look interested in the rapid-fire voice of the auctioneer or the bids criss-crossing the crowded room. There was a compelling stillness about him that made her long to lift her head and gaze at him openly, letting her eyes linger on the breadth of his shoulders and the hard planes of his lean, tanned face. She needed to look at his mouth too, she thought desperately, staring hard at the chandelier. At first glance it had looked almost indecently perfect—the deeply indented upper lip sloping steeply upward from a full, sensual lower one—but she knew that if she looked again she might not be able to drag her eyes off him.

Maybe she knew him from somewhere?

Ha. Like she wouldn't remember a face like that.

Taking a deep, steadying breath Bella twisted her rolled-up auction programme between her hands and tried to redirect her thoughts, as the expensive therapist her brother Miles had insisted on finding for her had urged her to do. When she felt her emotions running high, threatening to overwhelm her, she was supposed to think of something calming. Obediently she tried the beach thing again.

He was still looking at her.

Surreptitiously she untucked her short bobbed hair from behind her ear and let it swing forward over her face in a dark curtain, shielding her from the impassive scrutiny of his stare. The problem was silver-sanded beaches were such a cliché, and if she ever found herself on one she'd no doubt be bored to tears. There had to be some difference between feeling calm and feeling half dead with boredom, didn't there?

It was a question she had asked herself repeatedly in the last five months.

Bella shifted restlessly on the hard auction room chair and unfurled her programme. Two lots to go. The wire work chandelier was dismissed in a crack of the gavel and an earthenware confit jar took its place. If she leaned forward she could just catch a glimpse of the porter waiting at the edge of the room, carrying a large, heavily framed painting. The painting that in a few minutes would hopefully be hers, and then she could leave the stuffy, overcrowded room and the unsettling…arousing stare of the stranger.

Which, she had to remind herself sternly, would be a *good* thing.

She fixed her eyes on the painting, trying to focus on the greyish rectangle of the house against its backdrop of green— anything to stop herself turning to look again at the man. This picture was completely and without a doubt the perfect present for Grandmère, and by bringing Bella to the auction rooms the very week that it had come up for sale it seemed that fate, for once, was on her side.

Although, actually, believing in fate was another habit she was supposed to be giving up. The expensive therapist said that it was important that she started to take responsibility for her own actions and reactions instead of blaming vague outside forces like fate or destiny. Or horoscopes. She sighed. It wasn't easy. In fact in her darker moments she worried that all those things she was trying to give up weren't so much habits as personality traits. Parts of herself.

What would be left afterwards?

The gavel dropped on the jar and Bella sat up. This was it. With a renewed sense of purpose and determination she kept her gaze averted from the dark stare of the stranger and focused all her attention on the auctioneer.

'Lot four-six-five,' he announced in a bored voice, as if he wasn't about to sell a momentous piece of Bella's family history. 'Charming amateur oil on canvas of a beautiful French manor house. Who'll start the bidding at twenty pounds?'

There was a shuffling of feet on the front row. A woman with dyed red hair raised her hand wearily.

'Twenty pounds at the front here. Thirty with you, sir…'

A rapid flurry of bids followed, raising the price to ninety pounds. Since leaving art college and going to work for Celia in her Notting Hill antique shop Bella had become something of an expert at auction tactics, and knew to wait for the right moment before joining the bidding. It came a second later when the auctioneer asked for a hundred pounds and the woman in the front row shook her head.

'A hundred pounds anywhere?'

Decisively, Bella raised her hand.

She was immediately outbid by a dealer she recognised two rows in front of her.

'One hundred and twenty?' asked the auctioneer. Bella nodded, and could have shouted with elation when she saw the dealer give a cursory shake of his head as the auctioneer upped the bid.

'One hundred and twenty pounds then, with the dark-haired young lady. Going once at one hundred and twenty…'

Bella thrust her hands into the pockets of her black linen jacket and crossed her fingers so tightly that it hurt. She couldn't afford to go much higher.

'Going twice…'

Just get on with it… she begged silently.

'For the third and final—' The auctioneer broke off in surprise. 'Sir? Just in time, thank you. That's one hundred and thirty pounds from you, sir?'

Bella didn't have to look to know who had made the bid.

Somehow she just managed to bite back the extremely un-calm shriek of frustration that sprang to her lips. Glaring down at the floor, she uncrossed her fingers and balled them into tight fists. There was no point in resorting to superstitious good luck charms in a situation like this.

No.

This called for a skilful combination of bluff and bravery.

Tipping her head back she resisted the temptation to turn and fix the man with a death stare, instead focusing all her attention on assuming an attitude of supreme confidence, tinged with a hint of bored irritation. She'd seen this happen before. Utter insouciance was key. She had to look as if she was buying at any price; as if she was the kind of woman who was used to getting what she wanted.

Fortunately, there was no time to dwell on the bitter irony of that.

'One forty.'

Was that really her voice? Excellent. She actually sounded as if she knew what she was doing, and the realization brought a small smile to her face.

The moment of euphoria was very short-lived; his response was instant.

'Two hundred.'

Feeling her mouth fall open in helpless and no doubt deeply unattractive outrage, Bella couldn't stop her head from being pulled round in the direction of his voice. It was low and husky and completely indifferent—in fact, everything she had intended to convey herself, only genuine. He was looking straight at her.

She felt herself stiffen as her eyes locked with his.

'Miss? Do I have two ten?'

For a second Bella had forgotten about the auctioneer. And the picture. In fact, in that moment she would have been hard pushed to remember her own name. The man's eyes were dark—incredibly dark—and even at this distance she could detect a dangerous glitter in their depths. As she stared at him she saw one of his eyebrows move upwards a fraction. Questioningly. Challengingly.

'*Yes.*'

'Two ten with the—'

'Three hundred.'

Bella closed her eyes for a second as the man's voice cut through the auctioneer's patter. He said the words quietly, almost apologetically, as if her defeat was a foregone conclusion. But there was boredom and an edge of impatience there too, and she sensed that he wanted this whole business over and done with as quickly as possible.

'Three ten.'

The words were out of her mouth before she could stop them. It was futile—that much was obvious from the impeccable cut of his dark suit and the indefinable aura of wealth that enveloped him like expensive cologne. But his palpable indifference caused a sensation like a thousand red-hot needles piercing her skin.

He'd barely even glanced at the painting. He couldn't want it as she wanted it. Which left the possibility that he was doing this just to annoy her, and two could definitely play at that game.

'Five.'

'Sir?' The auctioneer was flustered by this unexpected turn of events and his sudden loss of control. 'Is that three hundred and fifty-five?'

'Five hundred.'

His mouth was quite incredible, she thought distractedly. It was a good thing his chin was exceptionally firm and square as his lips were so full and finely shaped they were almost feminine. As she watched they twitched into a smile which he quickly suppressed. It was as if he was enjoying some kind of private joke.

With her.

She felt as if she'd been hypnotized. Part of her mind remained aware, rational, firmly sceptical, while the rest of her threw off all inhibition and common sense and plunged into the thrill of the unknown without hesitation.

A ripple of interest ran through the room, like a sudden sharp breeze in a still summer field. Bella could feel eyes on her as people in the rows in front of her turned round to look. Only the man leaning against the wall remained supremely unruffled, his gaze fixed on hers, his face an impassive mask that was almost insolent.

Adrenalin burned and fizzed in Bella's veins. Tearing her gaze away from the stranger, she found the painting again. She had learned enough in the two years before she dropped out of her course at art school to be well aware that this was not an exceptional piece—there was a heavy-handed, painstaking quality about it that strictly limited its value. But it was the subject that mattered. This anonymous, half-forgotten painting depicted her grandmother's ancestral home. It was part of her heritage, and the thought filled her with renewed purpose.

'Five hundred and fifty.'

As if in slow motion she turned back to look at him, and saw his shoulders rise and fall slightly as he sighed. 'Six hundred.'

'Six fifty.'

'Seven hundred.'

There was something mesmerising about his voice and the dark, dark eyes that never wavered from her face. Bella shivered. This wasn't about oil on canvas. Or cash. This was personal.

'Seven hundred and fifty.'

The numbers had no meaning. The rest of the room could have dissolved in a heap of ashes for all she cared. Darkness gathered and swirled in her head, and through it all she could see, all she was aware of, was the man standing a few feet away from her, his eyes searing into hers. She felt the colour rising into her cheeks and ran her tongue over lips that felt dry and oddly swollen. Suddenly she was unbearably hot, as if the blood in her veins had been heated slowly over a low flame.

Hastily she shrugged off her jacket, letting it fall onto the chair behind her and revealing the sober little black dress she wore beneath. She had lost all sense of time. Only the thud of her heart marked each passing second as she stared at him. His hair was dark too, an untamed halo of curls, like a knight crusader. Or a gypsy...or... Or a pirate. His mouth, she saw now, had a brutal sensuality about it that made her think of plunder, and was entirely at odds with the crisp perfection of his bespoke suit. The expression *a wolf in sheep's clothing* drifted though her dazed, distracted mind.

He lifted his head, tilting it back against the wall, but still his eyes pinned her to the spot like a butterfly in a case. Slowly, deliberately, hardly moving those beautiful lips, he spoke with a light foreign inflection that was straight from every clichéd feminine fantasy, and he seemed to address her and her alone.

'One thousand pounds.'

Bella couldn't breathe.

'Miss?' The auctioneer's voice was stiff with surprise, and it seemed to be coming from a long way away. 'Any advance on one thousand? One thousand and ten?'

A terrible, languid recklessness stole through her. This must be what it felt like to jump from a plane, in the moment before the parachute unfurled: dizzying, terrifying, yet strangely peaceful. There was nothing to do but give in to the feeling, the irresistible pull of invisible forces beyond all control.

The painting was lost; that much was certain. There was no way she could compete. But there was more at stake now, and she wanted to push him just that little bit further, break through that infuriating, intriguing, madly provocative calm. She wanted to make him *feel* something. Even if it was only anger…

Defiantly she met his gaze in a look of silent, brazen challenge.

'Yes. One thousand and *five* pounds.'

With an inner smile of triumph she waited for him to come back, upping the price. The room was very still.

'Sir? One thousand and ten?'

The stranger's eyes held her own, then with agonizing slowness travelled downwards. Her throat felt as if it was full of cement, and through the panicky darkness that gathered at the edges of her vision she thought she registered the slowly spreading smile on his lips. Then, as if from a great distance, through veils of horror and disbelief Bella saw him shake his head.

Her stomach tightened reflexively, as if she'd just been punched, and all the air was driven from her lungs in an instant. Her mouth opened in shock. Through the swirling haze of horror she was aware only of his eyes. Amusement and triumph shone in their dark depths.

'One thousand and five pounds, then.' The auctioneer's gavel hovered. 'All finished at one thousand and five…? Going once…'

With contemptuous grace the man levered himself up from the wall and stepped forward. His gaze was still locked on her, but suddenly all the amusement had gone from it.

'Second time at one thousand and five…'

Bella's heart raced and her lips felt numb and bloodless. She was suddenly horribly afraid that she might faint, and was just stumbling blindly to her feet when she saw the man give the auctioneer a curt nod.

'Back with you, sir, at one thousand and ten?' asked the auctioneer.

He nodded again, and turned away from her. Bella sucked in a wild gulp of air. The sharp rap of the auctioneer's gavel shattered the bubble of unreality in her head, and broke the spell. Ducking her head, she pushed past the rows of curious onlookers and fled, too shattered by the emotions still rampaging through her to even feel relieved.

Eyes narrowed speculatively, Olivier Moreau watched her leave.

Interesting, he thought grimly. *Very, very interesting.* On several levels.

Notoriously cynical and quickly bored, he wasn't a man whose interest was easily captured. But by offering approximately ten times too much for an anonymous painting that could be described, at best, as average, she'd got it.

And the hectic sparks in her wide, dark eyes interested him too. She'd wanted that painting very much—enough to almost lose all sense of rationality in the process. She'd been out of control there for a moment and it had scared her. He'd seen it, sensed it.

The thing that interested him most was *why?*

She'd been in such a hurry to leave that she'd left her jacket lying on the chair, and on his way out he leaned over and scooped it up. It was of soft black linen, and as he held it he caught a soft breath of jasmine in its folds which caught him unawares and re-kindled the spark of desire that had been smouldering in the darkness inside him since the moment he'd first seen her.

At the porter's desk he handed over his bidding number and a thick wedge of banknotes. Waiting for his receipt, he looked down at the linen jacket in his hand, noticing, with a faint, sardonic smile, the very exclusive designer label in the back. Very grown-up, he thought idly, picturing it lying against the creamy skin of her neck. Very expensive, but disappointingly conservative and predictable. He would have liked to see her in something more individual.

And what an enticing carnival of vivid images *that* thought introduced…

He crushed the fabric back into one hand, decisively squashing a wicked picture of dark, shining hair against crimson silk as he walked out into the humid London afternoon.

It had been a summer of seemingly endless rain, and once again the sky was low and sullen, but Olivier barely noticed as he stood at the top of the steps. He felt restless and unsettled, as if something momentous was about to happen; something he hadn't quite planned for.

Maybe it was the painting, he mused grimly. Maybe this was it—the one he'd been looking for all these years.

Or maybe it was the girl.

* * *

Stopping dead in the middle of the pavement, Bella swore succinctly as she realised that she'd left her jacket behind in the auction room.

Knickers.

She was about to turn round when she hesitated. So what if the jacket was Valentino, and it belonged to her grandmother? So what if the heavens were about to open and she was only wearing a flimsy black dress? She should have been home ages ago—Miles always rang to check that she'd got back all right, and he'd worry if she wasn't there when he called, so really she should hurry...

She didn't move, paralysed by indecision and by the humiliating realization that her reluctance to go back to the auction house had nothing to do with lack of time and far more to do with lack of courage. Defiantly she turned round and began to retrace her steps as frustration swelled inside her, making the back of her throat prickle and her eyes sting. Now would be an excellent time to burst into tears, but unfortunately crying was another thing she'd given up, along with believing in fate and letting her emotions completely get the better of her.

Well, she'd certainly slipped up there. Big style. Her emotions had just had a field day, and all because of a dark-eyed glance from a good-looking man.

Except it hadn't been just a glance, had it? It had been an open challenge, a direct invitation, an intimate caress. Remembering it now made the skin on the back of her neck tingle as every tiny hair rose and shivered. She thought of those eyes, the measuring way they had lingered on her face, assessing her, then their speculative swoop over her body. She had felt more alive in that moment than in all the dead days of the past five empty months put together.

Life had felt full of excitement and possibility again.

She squeezed her eyes tight shut, trying to summon up that

damned white sandy beach as a vortex of unwelcome emotion opened up in front of her. Instead she saw dark eyes, a full, beautiful mouth. With a harsh sound of frustration she opened up her eyes again.

The image remained. Only now it was even more disturbing for being real.

'Don't tell me—you're trying to remember where you left this?'

The man from the auction room was standing a few feet away from her, a smile of sardonic amusement on his face, her jacket held in his outstretched hand. Bella's cheeks flamed. How long had he been watching her standing in the middle of the street with her eyes closed? He must think she was a complete headcase.

Which was something she usually preferred to conceal...

Hiding her embarrassment behind a screen of chilly hauteur, she snatched the jacket. 'I see. Not content with taking my painting, you also want my clothes now?'

It was a ridiculous thing to say. *Ridiculous.* What Miles would call 'a Bella classic'. The man laughed.

'That depends. Were you thinking of taking anything else off?'

Hot, treacherous, forbidden desire instantly shot through the shame, dissolving the carefully assembled shreds of Bella's self-control like Cinderella's dress on the stroke of midnight. She opened her mouth to make a stinging retort, but for a split second found herself speechless with resentment that he had managed so effortlessly to disturb her careful equilibrium. And then, of course, sense reasserted itself and she knew that any kind of emotional response would be a mistake.

Waves... White sandy beach...

With a huge effort she swallowed back the tide of wonderful, terrible words that threatened to flood from her and hid them behind a small, cold smile.

'Of course not. Thank you for picking it up. Now, if you don't mind I'm late and I have to hurry…'

Without looking up at him again she made to turn and walk away, wanting only to distance herself physically from the disturbing, charismatic pull of his presence and reassemble her defences, regain her comfortable numbness. But as she did so he reached out and took her arm, and the sensation of his fingers against her bare skin was like an electric shock. It ricocheted through her, making her flinch.

'Wait,' he said quietly. 'You said "my painting". In what way is that painting yours?'

Rigid with discomfort, his fingers still clasped around her arm, Bella looked down. 'It isn't,' she said stiffly. 'I'm sorry, that was a stupid thing to say. The painting's yours now. I know that.'

'But you're not happy about it, are you?'

She didn't reply. His voice was very low and, even standing in the middle of the street with traffic roaring past them along Piccadilly, disturbingly intimate. He shifted his position slightly, so that he was standing right in front of her, and she could see nothing but the solid wall of his chest. It was hard. Broad. Real. Very real. His fingers were still clasped around her arm; not too tightly, but she felt powerless to break away.

'You wanted it very much,' he said quietly. It was a statement, not a question.

'Yes,' she whispered.

'Why?'

'It's…nice,' Bella said tonelessly, thinking of calm, neutral things. Not thinking of his mouth, or how it would feel to kiss it.

'*Nice?*' Letting go of her arm, he took a step backwards and made a sharp expression of disgust. 'The hell it is.'

'I beg your pardon?

Olivier looked at her narrowly. Close up she had the kind of flawless, upmarket beauty that left him cold: short, glossy hair the colour of cherished old mahogany, skin like vanilla ice cream. Earlier on, in the auction room, he had thought he sensed a rawness and a passion in her which intrigued and excited him, but now he saw he'd been wrong. There was nothing but good breeding and good bones.

'You don't have to be an art expert to see that it's rubbish,' he said brutally. 'It's not worth a quarter of the hugely inflated price I just paid for it.'

That seemed to ignite some spark within her again. 'Then why did you bother?' she flared. 'Why couldn't you just let me have it? I'm not remotely interested in what it's worth or how collectable it is. I wanted it for reasons that have nothing to do with *money*.'

'Meaning?'

Her chin rose an inch. 'My grandmother grew up in the house in the picture. That's why I wanted it.'

The sky had darkened, and a warm breeze shivered through the leaves of the trees in the park opposite as the first drops of rain splashed onto the hot pavement. Everything was suddenly very still, as if the regular spin of the world had faltered for a second or two. Olivier almost wanted to reach out to hold on to something to steady himself as for the briefest moment the iron self-control, the bedrock of his being, shivered and shifted.

He took a slow breath in and summoned a bland smile to his stiff face. It felt like ice cracking on a frozen lake.

'Really? And your name is…?

'Bella. Bella Lawrence.'

Lawrence. Hearing the name was like a shot of adrenalin: painful, sickening, but exhilarating. He gritted his teeth, scrutinizing her. 'Well, Bella, what a…*coincidence* that you found a picture of it. You must have been thrilled.'

If she noticed the acid in his tone she didn't react. Nothing disturbed the blankness of that porcelain-pretty face. 'Yes,' she said sweetly, 'particularly since it's her birthday tomorrow and it would have been a perfect present.' She flashed him a saccharine smile. 'Obviously I didn't bargain on some millionaire city boy coming in at the last minute and paying silly money for it, so I'll just have to think again.'

Millionaire city boy? She'd underestimated him considerably. And because she was a Lawrence that stung.

She turned to go, but he had no intention of letting her disappear yet.

'What makes you think I'm a millionaire city boy?'

He didn't move. He didn't even raise his voice, but she turned back to him and Olivier felt a lick of triumph. As her eyes skimmed over him he took his phone from his inside pocket, barely glancing at it as he speed-dialled. Bella Lawrence shrugged.

'The suit. The shoes. The arrogance. Am I right?'

'Sort of.' Without taking his eyes from hers, he gestured with a terse movement of his head to a gleaming dark green Bentley that was just pulling up at the kerbside. 'Can I offer you a lift anywhere?'

Her eyebrows rose. 'Very impressive,' she said sarcastically. 'So you're half millionaire city boy, half magician. What else can you do?'

He gave her a lethal smile. 'Unfortunately, Mademoiselle Lawrence, my talents are too numerous to list now, while we're in grave danger of getting soaked to the skin and I'm late for a meeting. But if you'd like to get into the car I'd be only too happy to enlighten you.'

He opened the car door and stood back. The rain was falling harder now, releasing the scent of hot asphalt and damp earth and making the skin on her bare arms glisten, but she didn't move.

'No, thank you,' she said politely. 'I don't think it would be a good idea.'

'Ri-ight.' His fingers drummed an impatient beat on the roof of the car. 'And I suppose you'd argue that choosing to get completely and unnecessarily soaked is a stroke of genius, would you?' He sighed and stood back. 'Look, you said yourself that you're in a hurry—if it makes you feel better you can have the car to yourself. My office is just around the corner in Curzon Street. I'll walk. Just tell Louis where you want to go.'

He took a couple of steps backwards, still watching her, silently willing her to accept the offer. He would find out where she lived eventually, but it would be so much easier to do it this way. The pavement was virtually empty now, as everyone with any sense had rushed to shelter in doorways or disappeared into the dark mouth of the tube. Bella Lawrence stood beside the open door of the Bentley in her expensive black dress, her hair slick with water.

She frowned suspiciously. 'Why?'

'The painting—let's just say it's the least I can do. Please.'

She glanced up at the angry sky and hesitated. And then, bristling with resentment and indignation, slipped into the car and leaned forward to pull the door briskly shut. She didn't look at him.

'My pleasure,' he murmured sarcastically to himself as the car drew smoothly away from the kerb and was swallowed up by the Friday afternoon traffic.

Though 'pleasure' wasn't quite the right word for it, he reflected as he thrust his hands into his pockets and strode through the rain.

Satisfaction.

That was it.

CHAPTER TWO

GENEVIEVE DELACROIX'S face was pale, delicately tinted with a faint rose-pink blush, as if in the aftermath of passion, and her rosy lips were curved in a lazy smile of repletion. Reclining on the velvet-draped couch, she was completely naked, apart from a large and heavily jewel-encrusted gold cross hanging on a length of red velvet ribbon around her neck.

Her eyes, dark blue and watchful, seemed to bore into Olivier's back as he stood at the glass wall of his apartment, looking down over the most expensive view in London. Eight storeys below him cars sailed noiselessly along Park Lane, and above him planes bound for Heathrow studded the indigo sky with flashing points of light, outshining the stars. But Olivier noticed none of this. The image of the painting swam in front of him, superimposed on the glittering cityscape in the polished sheet of glass.

His instinct about the 'charming amateur painting' in the saleroom had been correct. Although it was unsigned, its subject matter—Le Manoir St Laurien—and the distinctively painstaking style of the brushwork had left him in no doubt that it had been painted by his father.

But Julien Moreau was no amateur. Had things been different he would have been one of the most important painters of his generation.

Olivier took a gulp of cognac from the glass in his hand, draining half the contents in a single mouthful, and then, steeling himself as if against a blow, he turned to face the picture behind him. The one that had lain hidden beneath the other work.

La Dame de la Croix.

For years he had searched for this painting. His contacts in the art world spread across the globe and encompassed all the major auction houses, galleries and collections, but since he knew that the portrait of Genevieve Delacroix was likely to have been concealed behind one of Julien's flawed, later attempts, his contacts had been of little help. He had tried to keep an eye on the catalogues of smaller salerooms, but it had been like searching for a needle in a haystack. The odds had been impossibly stacked against him.

And yet he had done it. The painting was here, propped up on a tall steel bar chair in front of him, as fresh and vivid as if the paint was still wet.

Olivier Moreau prided himself on his ability to achieve. He was a man who got what he wanted through a combination of intelligence, focus and ruthlessness, but he knew that none of that was enough to have pulled off today's coup.

That had been down to luck. Or maybe fate, or some long-overdue divine justice. Karma, some people might call it; after all, it was about time the mighty Lawrences were made to face up to what they'd done, and now the painting was back in his possession he could begin the process of exacting retribution.

He took another mouthful of cognac and let his gaze run speculatively over Genevieve Delacroix's luscious flesh. Hypothetically, in the long years when he had dreamed of recovering this picture, he had always imagined he would simply reveal it, and the shocking scandal behind it, to the world in the most high-profile and damaging way possible.

But now that didn't seem enough.

In his work Olivier operated on a principle of 'absolute return'. His success lay in his ability to exact profit—maximum profit—from every available opportunity, and in this instance fate had very kindly presented him with not one opportunity, but two. *La Dame de la Croix* and Bella Lawrence had both fallen into his lap on the same day. He wouldn't be the man he was if he let a chance like that pass without exploiting it to the full.

Fate…justice…karma—it hardly mattered what you called it. In truth they were all just euphemisms for revenge. The Lawrences didn't know it yet, but it was payback time.

An eye for an eye.

A tooth for a tooth.

A heart for a heart.

Genevieve Lawrence was standing in the hallway rearranging the flowers that had just been delivered by one of London's most exclusive florists when Bella came downstairs.

'Morning,' Bella said with an apologetic smile, kissing her grandmother's perfumed cheek.

Genevieve cast an amused glance at her little gold watch. 'Only just, *cherie*,' she said in her voice of silk and silver. It might have been a lifetime since the young Genevieve Delacroix had left France to marry the dashing and distinguished Lord Edward Lawrence, but her accent was still as strong as ever. 'I take it you slept well?'

'Yes, thanks,' Bella lied. There was no point in telling Genevieve that sleep had proved so elusive that she'd ended up sitting by the window and sketching in the moonlight. The man from the auction house, whose face was still so vivid in her mind, had proved frustratingly difficult to capture on paper. The sky had been streaked with pink when she'd finally given up trying and crawled back into bed. 'Is there still lots to do for tonight?'

Pulling a dripping long-stemmed lily from the vase, Genevieve sighed. 'There does seem to be a lot of last-minute things to attend to. For one thing, these flowers are all wrong. Now I remember why I haven't entertained like this since your grandfather died.'

Bella made a soft, sympathetic sound. After almost fifty years of marriage, Genevieve had been widowed two years ago. 'Will it be awful for you, to do it without him?'

'Awful? Not at all,' said Genevieve matter-of-factly, looking critically at the arrangement of lilies and white hydrangeas. She didn't elaborate, and Bella realised with a flicker of surprise how little she knew her grandmother. Up until five months ago she had been nothing but a remote, elegant figure who had always stood silently by Edward Lawrence's side: coolness and shade to the full-on dazzle of his forceful presence. It was only since Bella had come, at Miles's insistence, to live in the house in Wilton Square, following the business with Dan Nightingale, that she had begun to see the person behind the impeccable façade. And to like her.

'It is a shame that your mama and papa cannot be here, though,' Genevieve continued, adjusting a glossy, tropical-looking leaf. 'I had a call from your mother this morning to say there has been more trouble overnight and the diplomatic situation is too tense for your papa to leave just now.'

Bella was slightly ashamed at the relief that leapt within her. Used to being the invisible member of the dynamic and high-achieving Lawrence family, she had felt completely smothered by the attention which had been focused on her since the Dan Nightingale thing, and she had been dreading seeing her parents for the first time since it happened. Miles's stifling concern was quite enough to deal with.

'They must be very disappointed,' she said guiltily.

Genevieve gave a little lift of her narrow shoulders. 'You

know the Lawrence men, *cherie*. Work comes first. But we will manage without them, I dare say. Now—have you decided what you will wear tonight?'

Bella's eyes lit up. 'Well…I got this gorgeous little silk smock dress in Portobello Market the other day. It's bright red with fuchsia-pink flowers around the hem, with kind of pink sequins and gold embroidery on them…' The words came out in a rush of enthusiasm and her hands fluttered in the air, sketching fluid lines. 'And it's short—but not, you know, indecently short, and it's got this deep scooped neckline and sweet little sleeves…' The words petered out.

'It sounds fabulous, *cherie*.'

'Yes…' Subdued again, Bella paused. 'You know, I think maybe it would be better if I borrowed your black Balenciaga, though.'

Genevieve's fine eyebrows rose questioningly. 'Would it be foolish to ask why?'

'I think that Miles would rather I—I don't know…I think I should just keep it low key. After all that's happened…'

Picking at the spiky leaves of a discarded palm leaf, Bella didn't notice the concerned glance Genevieve cast her; however, she did detect the faint note of reproach in her grandmother's voice. 'Bella, *ma chère,* you cannot spend your life trying to be what your brother wants you to be.'

Bella gave a crooked smile. 'No, but perhaps I have less chance of messing up that way. After all, I made a huge fuss about being given the chance to be myself and live my own life, and look what happened.'

'You made a mistake,' said Genevieve mildly. 'Is that so bad?'

Bella's smile faded. The huge, marble-tiled hallway felt suddenly cold. 'Given that it could have caused a scandal which may have cost Papa *and* Miles their jobs, I think that's as bad as I'd like it to get,' she said quietly. Without realizing it she had completely stripped the palm frond, and its shredded leaves were scattered over the polished surface of the table. 'I don't want to make things any more difficult for Miles than I have already. It's a pretty important time for him just now, with the election coming up and everything, and the last thing he needs is his drop-out, headcase sister mucking things up for him again.'

'But, *cherie,* this is a private party for my birthday, not a political rally for Miles. You can wear what you like.'

'I know, but you have to admit, *Grandmère,* that you have some pretty influential friends. I think I should stay in the background as much as possible.' She gave a short laugh. 'In fact it would probably be better all round if I didn't come…'

She had been sweeping the torn leaves into a little pile, but now Genevieve stopped her, laying her hand over Bella's quite firmly. 'Stop this, Bella.'

'Sorry… It's not that I don't want to be there for your party, it's just that you have to admit I'm a bit of a liability,' Bella said lightly. She gave an awkward smile. 'Even Ashley, PR Genius and Totally Nice Person, would have her work cut out making an art school dropout, shop girl and psychiatrist's dream ticket seem like a political asset.'

'Oh, Bella,' Genevieve sighed. Suddenly she seemed very sad. 'You have such *talent*. If only you could see that.'

'For art,' said Bella soberly. 'That's all, and that avenue is fairly conclusively closed since—'

Genevieve cut her off. *'Non.* Not just for art. For empathy. For understanding people, and seeing through the façade to what lies beneath. For *loving.'*

Bella laughed, but there was a faint tinge of bitterness to it. 'I think Miles would say that's my problem, not my talent.'

'Non! Don't let him make you believe that!'

The sudden rawness in Genevieve's voice made Bella's heart miss a beat. Her words echoed for a moment round the grand room, seeming out of place amongst the gleaming marble and polished wood, the perfectly arranged Sèvres china and Georgian silver. The orchid she had been holding fell to the floor as Genevieve took Bella's hands in hers.

'I do not want to watch you throw away your happiness to appease your family. Please, *cherie,* tell me you won't. Don't make the same mistake that I made.'

As the car glided through the security cordon at the entrance to Wilton Square, the noise and activity of the city was left behind and Olivier felt as if he was entering a charmed world. Beyond the dark shapes of the trees in the central garden Genevieve Delacroix's ivory mansion blazed with light, and music spilled from windows which had been thrown open against the sticky air. The party had been going for an hour or so, and Olivier had timed his arrival carefully to allow him to slip in relatively unnoticed.

The enormous black front door was opened by a stiff-backed butler in white tie and tails, and Olivier handed over the gold-edged invitation he had managed to procure from a contact in the Treasury who owed him a favour. The butler took it with an impassive nod, gesturing for him to leave the gift he carried on a mahogany sideboard groaning under the weight of exquisitely wrapped parcels. Placing the painting of Le Manoir St Laurien, carefully reinserted into its frame, amongst them, Olivier followed the direction of the noise.

The spacious first-floor sitting room was packed with cabinet ministers, high-powered media figures and ancient aristocrats, and their loud, almost unintelligibly well-bred voices drifted assuredly above the music of the band downstairs. So this was the world of Bella Lawrence, he thought as his eyes moved around the elegant panelled room. Luxurious, expensive, exclusive… things that she no doubt took for granted and barely noticed. It was what she'd been born to.

Without being particularly conscious of it, he found his gaze skimming over the distinguished, easily recognizable faces of politicians and TV celebrities, searching for one face in particular. But the vicious kick of desire in the pit of his stomach when he saw her caught him off guard.

She was wearing another slim-fitting, severe black dress, which disguised rather than emphasised her figure, and high heels that made her endless legs seem as gracefully unsteady as a colt's. She carried a large plate of canapés, which she was offering to a noisy group of media types. Her face was hidden by the silken curtain of her hair, but there was a stiffness in the set of her shoulders and a downward tilt to her head that told him she wasn't smiling.

This was her world. So why did she look so out of place?

'Caviar blini?' he heard her murmur to a prominent TV news journalist, who took one without glancing at her or breaking off his conversation.

Eyes narrowed, Olivier watched.

Warm waves…sandy beach…top TV newsreader lying on it while I smash a plate of caviar blinis over his head…

Bella's smile was a painful rictus grin as she moved on, wondering how soon she could beat a hasty retreat to her room and curl up with a book. *Any time now,* she thought resignedly, *for all the notice anyone's taking of me.*

As she moved further into the room she could hear Miles's voice—confident, urbane, totally in command—and once again the randomness of the gene lottery was brought home to her. How could it be that he was so…*assured,* and she had never felt a moment's assurance in her whole life? She kept her head bowed, her back towards him, hoping to pass by unnoticed and be spared the inevitable embarrassment of being introduced to whichever political worthy he was talking to.

'Ah, Bella! There you are…I was just talking about you.'

If Bella had been wearing boots at that moment her heart would have sunk into the bottom of them. Fortunately, her shiny black high-heeled shoes were too tight to leave any room for anything else, so she summoned a smile and turned round.

'This is my little sister, Bella,' Miles said heartily to the vaguely familiar-looking man standing beside him. 'Named after the suffragette Christabel Pankhurst.'

Taking a caviar blini, the man smiled politely. 'Of course. And as one of the distinguished Lawrence family I imagine you're just as much of a trailblazer as your namesake?'

Bella felt her smile falter. *Oh, yes, absolutely*, she wanted to say. *I'm the first member of my family to fail at anything and become a dropout*. Just as she was wondering how to frame this sentence slightly more positively, the slim brunette at Miles's side stepped in.

'Bella's the artistic one in the family, Prime Minister. She's incredibly talented, so although Miles needs help to match a pair of socks, I actually have hope that we might just end up having children with a glimmer of creativity…'

Prime Minister. Oh, knickers. That was why she recognised him…

Bella cast a grateful glance at the girl who had spoken. Ashley McGarry was Miles's fiancée. She was also extremely gorgeous, owned her own incredibly successful PR firm and was just about the nicest person Bella knew. Which was good, because it would have been hard to forgive her for the gorgeousness and success otherwise.

'So, what kind of art do you do?' the Prime Minister asked her politely.

Bella squirmed. 'I paint furniture.'

The PM looked surprised. He'd clearly expected something a little more cutting edge. Ashley came to the rescue again. 'Bella has one of the most enviable jobs in London, working in a gorgeous shop in Notting Hill that sells French antiques and vintage stuff.' She turned to Bella with an encouraging smile. 'I went back the other day to see if that fabulous mirror was still there, but Celia had sold it. I was so disappointed.'

Don't worry,' said Bella. 'Her daughter's twins are due any minute, so she's asked me to do the autumn buying trip to France. I'm going to take her car and tour the markets around Paris, so I can look out for another one for you then.'

Miles looked up. 'You're going to France, Bella? On your own?'

Suddenly the atmosphere was very tense. Ashley laid a hand on Bella's arm but this time said nothing. Bella felt as if someone was slowly pouring cold porridge down her back. How could she be having this conversation now? *In front of the Prime Minister?*

'Yes, Miles,' she said miserably, looking at the floor. 'I'll be fine.'

'We'll talk about it later.'

'There's no need—I've said I'm going, and that's that.'

Miles turned back to the Prime Minister and said with forced cheerfulness, 'My sister hasn't been…well. She's still recovering and she needs keeping an eye on.'

It was too humiliating. Bella seemed to spend her whole life these days trying to forget what had happened, but it was impossible when to everyone else it was the single most significant thing about her. Speechless with suppressed rage, she whirled round, the plate clasped in front of her like a weapon, and walked straight into someone stepping towards her.

As if in slow motion she watched caviar blinis sail gracefully through the air and rain down all around her. The plate jolted against her hipbones, coming between her and the body of the man with whom she had collided. In a daze of embarrassment and misery she sank instantly to the floor and started to pick up scattered canapés, desperate to clear up the damage and get out.

The man she had bumped into dropped to his knees beside her.

'It's fine,' she muttered miserably, without looking up. 'Please don't bother. I can manage.'

'Leave it.'

His voice was very low, and very French. And very filled with barely suppressed anger.

She froze. Then, full of foreboding, she dragged her gaze upwards. Her indrawn breath made a little gasping sound. She was looking straight into the dark, gleaming eyes of the man from the auction house.

'Wh—what? I don't understand…' she whispered hoarsely. 'What are you doing here?'

'Taking you away.' Removing the plate from her hands, he put it on a side table and gently pulled her up. She was suddenly aware of Miles behind her, looking at her with obvious dismay that she'd managed to make a fool of herself again. She could hardly blame him. She was standing liberally smeared in first-class beluga caviar just a few feet away from the Prime Minister and some of the most important, most famous and influential people in the country.

And in front of possibly the best-looking man on the planet.

Without warning, hot tears stung her eyes, but before they spilled over she felt the man from the auction take her chin in his fingers and gently tilt her head up.

'Oh, no you don't, beauty. You're not going to cry,' he murmured as he bent towards her, and in a heartbeat his mouth closed over hers, warm and firm. For a second she felt herself stiffen, but her gasp of shock was lost in his kiss.

The bright, tasteful room full of people dissolved, the loud music of the band faded away, and along with it her shame and humiliation. She was in a dark, secret world of lips and hands, and the only sound was the frantic drumbeat of her heart. Or his heart. Or both together…

After a second, a minute, a lifetime, he lifted his head and with one hand in the small of her back moved his mouth to her ear.

'OK, *cherie,* smile nicely and head for the door.'

Bella opened her mouth to protest, but he swept his thumb swiftly across it.

'Don't speak,' he murmured huskily. 'Don't say a word. You can thank me later.'

CHAPTER THREE

OLIVIER followed her through the crowded room.

Already, he noticed, she was walking taller, holding her head higher. There was a provocative sway to her hips. In short, a glimmer of the brilliant spark he had noticed yesterday in the auction room had returned.

With just one kiss.

Dieu, what he would do to her with a whole night.

The thought brought the ghost of a smile to his set face. He had decided already that seducing Genevieve Lawrence's grand-daughter, sleeping with her, would be a matter of cold-blooded score-settling, but if the change he'd just witnessed was anything to go by it would almost be too pleasurable to count as vengeance.

How would it feel to touch the flesh that had been so forbidden to his father? How would it feel to possess such a price-less pearl...the daughter of the Delacroix dynasty...and then cast it away as if it were worthless? Would it make up for what they had done?

On the landing outside the sitting room she stopped and turned to him. There was a pink stain in her cheeks and an intense, almost feverish glitter in her eyes.

'Thank you? I'm supposed to thank you for this?' She looked down at herself. Beads of caviar gleamed darkly on the pale skin

of her arms and the ivory swell of her breast. 'Of *course*. Caviar body paint is *such* a good look…'

Olivier smiled lazily. She might be being sarcastic, but she was actually completely right. She looked good enough to eat. 'Believe me,' he drawled, 'it's a lot better than being completely humiliated in public by some overbearing bastard treating you like a child.'

'Do you mind?' she gasped. 'That was my brother!'

'And that makes it all right for him to treat you like that?' Olivier asked coolly.

'He's protective. He just—' Bella broke off, shaking her head in confusion. 'Look, I don't know what this has to do with you…'

'I don't like bullying. Now, which is your room?'

'Why?' she demanded.

He paused, looking at her thoughtfully. Standing there with her eyes sparking with fury she looked oddly sweet, and he couldn't help but admire her defiance. The prospect of seducing her was like a sudden and unexpected blow to the stomach. 'Let's just say I don't like people who use their natural advantages to repress people who don't have the same power,' he said quietly.

She laughed suddenly: a short, joyful peal that broke the tension. 'I didn't mean that.' She looked up at him and their gazes locked. 'I meant, why do you want to know which is my room?'

'Because I think you need to get out of that dress.'

The sparkling laughter faded from her eyes, and was replaced by something much more intense.

Gently, not wanting to frighten her, he reached out and cupped her breast in the flat of his hand, feeling the ripeness and heat of her skin through the severe black crêpe. A small shiver ran through her. Slowly, lazily, he ran his thumb over the bare skin above the low-cut neckline of the dress where her cleavage spilled out, scooping up black beads of caviar that glistened against the creamy flesh. Her eyes stayed fixed to his the entire time, and he saw the momentary flicker of her eyelids at his touch.

Removing his hand, he put his thumb to his lips and sucked off the caviar.

She drew in a soft, shuddering breath. 'Up there,' she said in a low voice. 'My room is up there.'

'Then allow me…' Olivier almost expected her to protest as he took her hand and led her to the stairs, but passively she allowed him to lead her. Even so, he had the impression that a fierce battle was going on beneath that graceful exterior. This little rich girl had been brought up to be polite and well behaved, but all the etiquette and good breeding couldn't quite conceal the wildness that heated her blue-tinged blood.

Just like her Grandmother. Just like the original *Dame de la Croix*.

He followed her across the thickly carpeted upper landing. She opened a door, revealing a pretty room with a window set into its sloping roof. Outside a blue August twilight was gathering over the treetops in the residents' garden opposite, casting deep, inky shadows in the room. Just inside the door she stopped and turned to him.

'Wait!' She looked agitated. 'I don't know anything about you. I don't even know your name…'

'Olivier Moreau.' Solemnly he held out his hand and said with a tiny hint of sarcasm, 'Millionaire city boy.'

He was rewarded with a smile so brief it had disappeared before it was properly there. 'You said I was only half right about that. Who are you really?'

'I'm a hedge fund manager.'

'What does that mean?'

He paused, weighing up how to answer. 'I buy and sell… things.'

'What things?'

He shrugged. 'Anything. But I like dealing in the complex, indefinable things best. Rain, air quality, confidence…'

'Or other people's heritage?' she added bitingly.

He acknowledged the dig with a small smile. 'Exactly. As long as it gives me a good return on the investment. What else can I tell you? I'm French, but I've been based in London for the last four years. I collect art. I'm not married and I have no children. Is there anything else you'd like to know?'

'Why you came here tonight.'

She walked away from him into the room, but he stayed where he was, lounging easily against the doorframe. He didn't want to rush her, or pressure her. There was no need.

'I wanted to see you again,' he said simply. 'After yesterday.'

She was standing by the wardrobe with her back to him, her head bent as she fumbled with the buttons on the back of the dress. In the melting blue light her neck was as pale and delicate as the petals of a lily.

'What for?'

Her directness was unexpected, but Olivier admired her for it. Slowly he moved across the twilit room, desire licking through him in instant, automatic response as he reached out to help her. His libido obviously had little respect for history or family loyalty, he thought dryly, noticing that she stiffened slightly as he slid the button from its tiny satin loop.

His fingers moved down to the second button. 'I wanted to give you what's rightfully yours.'

'The painting?' There was a pause as the dress slid from her shoulders, revealing the flawless expanse of her bare back. It glimmered milk-white in the moonlight for a moment, and then she turned round so she was facing him.

'Of course.'

In her 'take-me' heels, with the caviar-smeared black dress clutched against her breasts, she looked dishevelled and wanton, but when she spoke the icy hauteur in her voice shattered the enchantment.

'No, thanks.'

He felt an uncomfortable jolt of surprise but instantly concealed it, looking at her steadily. 'Why not? You said it was your grandmother's house. If that's the case then she should have it.'

'It's too expensive.'

He moved slowly towards her, genuine interest gleaming in his eyes. Having a woman turn down a gift on the grounds that it was 'too expensive' was a bit like having a goldfish decide against a bowl of water on the basis that it was too wet. He was intrigued.

'I thought you said yesterday that you didn't care how much it was worth?'

'I did,' she said with cold disdain. 'But that's irrelevant now. You're a businessman, Mr Moreau, and I assume that part of your success rests on knowing your market. You no doubt think that all this—' she made a sweeping gesture with one arm, causing a corner of the dress to fall down, revealing a tantalizing glimpse of voluptuous flesh '—means I'm some wealthy, profligate trustafarian, and you can sell the painting to me at a profit because you know how much I wanted it.' She shook her head emphatically. 'Well, I just hope that your projections in the boardroom are a lot more accurate than the ones you've made about me, because that's a huge miscalculation. It makes no difference how much I want the painting because I can't *afford* it.'

She stopped, her chin raised in awkward defiance, her dark hair framing a face that burned with fury and bitterness and passion. For a moment neither of them spoke, and above the distant thud of the band Olivier could hear Bella's laboured breathing. In the half-light her shoulders looked fragile and translucent as they rose and fell rapidly.

'Great speech,' he said dryly after a long pause. 'However, completely unnecessary. I said I came to *give* it to you.'

'Why? Why would you do that?'

The space between them seemed to pulse with possibility.

Watching her closely, Olivier could see that the hostility that crackled around her like static was due in part to a deep-seated uncertainty. Insecurity, perhaps. Having seen her arrogant, over-bearing brother at work, it wasn't hard to work out where that had come from.

He gently lifted the fallen edge of her dress, tucking it back in place and hiding the ivory swell of her breast, careful not to let his fingers brush her skin.

She shivered.

'You want it,' he said simply, looking at her thoughtfully. He saw the heat flare in her eyes and knew she had all but forgotten, as he had intended her to, that he was referring to the painting.

He turned, hiding his slight smile of triumph, and walked casually across the room. 'I left it downstairs. I hope your grand-mother likes it,' he said, and closed the door quietly behind him.

Going down the wide stairs, he counted each step. Would she come after him before he reached the first floor, or would she manage to hold out for longer and leave it until he'd reached the hallway?

There was, of course, no question that she would come after him.

He reached the front door and, ignoring the imperious man-servant who had welcomed him on the way in, stepped out into the warm evening. He had to hand it to her. She was pushing it to the limit. Unhurriedly he crossed the empty street to where his car was waiting, and was just reaching out a hand to the open the door when he heard the clatter of her heels on the marble floor behind him. At the sound of her voice he found he was smiling.

'Wait—please wait!'

He arranged his face into an expression of bland enquiry before he turned round.

She had put on a short dress of vivid scarlet silk, loose and flowing like a smock, and as she ran down the steps towards him the silk rippled against the curves of her body like water cascading over a statue in a fountain. The transformation from the bland, dutiful girl he had watched up there in the drawing room to this vibrant beauty was breathtaking. It was as if she had been brought back to life.

She came to an abrupt halt by the pillared entrance portico.

'I'm sorry for being so suspicious and cynical,' she said, and her voice vibrated with suppressed emotion. She was trembling. 'I've learned the hard way, I'm afraid. It made me forget that there are good people out there too. I'm sorry, please—forgive me.'

Olivier found himself taking a couple of steps towards her, so he was standing in the middle of the carless road.

'Apology accepted.' He raised an eyebrow. 'Was there anything else?'

'Yes.' Keeping her chin held high, she came down the steps to where he stood. Her eyes flashed with feeling. 'I never said thank you.'

The height of her heels meant that she didn't have to stretch upwards very far to press a kiss on his cheek, but they also made her unsteady. As she leaned over she wobbled slightly, and Olivier found himself grasping her arms as the warmth and softness of her lips met his skin.

He didn't let go of her straight away. 'There's no need to thank me,' he said with a trace of mockery. 'According to you the painting was morally yours all along.'

She gave a breathy laugh and looked down as he let her go. 'All right, then…not just for the painting. For extracting me from an extremely embarrassing situation, and making my brother see I'm not a child any more.'

Olivier glanced up at the row of tall windows behind their elegant wrought-iron balconies on the first floor. Miles was still there, and as Olivier watched he glanced down. Olivier felt a small dart of triumph as he saw the expression of anger and dis-approval on Miles Lawrence's handsome face.

'It was my pleasure,' he said dryly.

'He only does it because he cares, but unfortunately it's a very thin line between being caring and being controlling—especially where my love-life is concerned. No one is ever going to be *good enough* for his little sister, of course...'

Loathing rose up in Olivier's throat as she said that. *Not good enough.* Times had changed, the world had moved on, but it seemed that Miles Lawrence still held fast the same outdated, elitist principles of his forebears. The principles that had ruined Julien Moreau's life.

'Charming,' he murmured sardonically. Bella jumped slightly as he trailed a caressing finger down her cheek, adding lightly, 'Don't look now, but he's watching.'

Her eyes widened a little as understanding dawned. It was like dipping a brush of black ink into clear water, Olivier thought idly as the darkness of her pupils spread and deepened. Her head tilted back a little and her lips parted as slowly, deliberately, he bent his head and their lips met in the lightest butterfly touch.

He had her.

Lifting his hand to cup her face, he dipped his head again and closed his mouth over hers. His fingers slipped into the silk of her hair, and he felt her tongue dart between his open lips. He had her, and tasting Delacroix flesh was every bit as easy and as sweet as he'd anticipated.

Bella slid her hands inside his dinner jacket, placing her palms flat against his ribs where she could feel the steady rhythm of his heart. His body was warm, reassuringly solid, and the expensive, dry, masculine scent of him filled her head and blotted out the city smells of dust and diesel and night-scented stock from the square's garden. She felt as if she was melting, and the violent trembling that had gripped her since she had run down the stairs after him eased, replaced by a delicious languor like honey in her veins.

The summer evening enfolded them as they stood alone in a

halo of light from the windows, and the music of the band eddied around them. They were playing a mellow, dreamy song, and Bella felt her hips undulating lazily beneath Olivier's warm hand.

Desire beat an indolent tattoo in her blood. She felt heavy with it, drenched and pulsing, as if there was an unhurried inevitability about it. The panic that she had felt before had completely disappeared. Suddenly she didn't care what her family thought of her. What must Miles be saying now? That she was irresponsible…?

Olivier's mouth moved to her cheek, the hollow beneath her ear, the curve of her neck.

Mmm…yes. Irresponsible, definitely…

She slid her hands over his shoulders, arching her back as his lips raised goosebumps up her arms.

Impulsive?

Oh, yes. There were impulses that she had barely dared to imagine raging through her like forked lightning, and she wanted nothing more than to give into each and every one of them.

Easily led…

'Oh…'

She felt a sharp stab of dismay as Olivier lifted his head and pulled back from her a little. Her skin tingled and sang with the need to feel his lips against it again.

The expression on his face was impossible to read as he looked down at her, but his voice was wry and slightly mocking. 'Do you think that showed him?'

For a moment Bella didn't understand what he meant, and then disappointment and shame hit her as she remembered that this was just an act to annoy Miles. She gave a shaky laugh, desperate to make light of the terrifying and utterly genuine lust that rampaged through her.

'Not sure…' she said lightly. 'Maybe sex on the back seat of your car…just to be completely certain he got the message that I'm a big girl now…?'

There was a part of her—a distant, dutiful part—that was completely horrified by what she'd just said but was helpless to intervene. The expensive therapist would have a fit, but Bella felt as if she had torn off a mask and was finally revealing herself. It felt good. She was tired of being invisible; she wanted to be noticed.

His mouth curved into a lazy, wicked smile that simultaneously dazzled her and made her squirm with painful, pulsing longing.

'I'm sure my driver would enjoy that,' he murmured.

She met his gaze and smiled challengingly. 'I didn't mean with him.'

For a moment neither of them moved. The laughter that had been bubbling inside her was obliterated by a tide of drenching urgency. From behind them, in the house, there was a ripple of applause as the band finished the song, and then silence.

His eyes were so dark it was impossible to see where the pupil ended and the iris began. The band started up again, in a persuasive flourish of strings. As if in a dream she stroked the flat of her hand down the silk lapel of his jacket, swaying slightly against him.

Unsmiling, Olivier held out his hand.

With slow deliberation Bella touched her palm to his. For a moment they stood there like that, while the music curled around them, and then Bella let her fingers close around his. His hand felt big in hers, strong and unbending, and as she moved towards him his other hand came up to her waist, bunching up the thin silk as it slid across her back. She held his shoulder, but despite the formality of their position she couldn't help tilting her pelvis towards him, arching her back so her hipbones bumped against his.

And then they were dancing. His hooded eyes glittered down at her, but his face remained completely still.

He was guiding her steps gently, expertly, and the click of her heels echoed dully off the high buildings around them as they swayed against each other in the empty street. Above them the sky had darkened to a rich sapphire-blue, and the sounds of the city seemed very far away. There was just the music and the presence of this man, this stranger with his dark, hypnotic eyes and his aura of quiet, persuasive strength.

He had the stillest face she had ever seen, she thought hazily. His exceptional beauty concealed everything, like armour. She had a sudden fierce, searing need to get past it to the man beneath.

'I have to go.'

His words cut crudely through her thoughts. He was pulling away from her, distancing himself, and she felt instantly desolate.

'Why? Where are you going?'

'I'm due at a reception at the Tate. I've donated a picture to their forthcoming exhibition, and it's the private view tonight. I have to be there.' He hesitated, looking at her measuringly. 'But you could come with me, if you'd like to?'

'I can't. My grandmother—it's her party and—'

She broke off. Miles had appeared in the doorway, his face a scowling mixture of irritation and concern. 'Bella, come back inside at once,' he said with barely concealed impatience, then gave a nervous half laugh. 'That dress is completely inadequate for hanging about outside. You'll catch your death of cold.'

Olivier's eyes were on her. She could feel their dark, silent challenge. She looked from him to Miles, and was suddenly aware that her big brother, who had always seemed so omnipotent, so completely in control, was *afraid*. And then she looked back to where Olivier stood, strong and certain, and Genevieve's words from that morning came back to her.

Don't throw away your happiness to appease your family.

She would understand.

Hesitantly she walked forward towards Olivier, and took his hand, feeling his power give her strength. 'I'd like to come with you—if I may?' At his brief nod of assent she turned back to Miles, and so missed the dark gleam of triumph in Olivier Moreau's eyes.

CHAPTER FOUR

'I'M GLAD you changed your mind.'

Olivier kept his gaze fixed casually ahead. Bella seemed to have pressed herself into the furthest corner of the car seat and was sitting stiffly, her hands tucked between her thighs and the soft leather upholstery.

'I don't think Miles would say the same thing. I'm going to have a lot of explaining to do later.'

The easy sensuality of a few minutes ago had melted away, and replacing it was that dull listlessness which he'd noticed yesterday in the street and earlier at the party. It exasperated him beyond belief.

'Why?'

'He'll be worried about me.'

Olivier's jaw tensed. 'Of course,' he said sourly. 'I'm not *good enough* to take his little sister out.'

She shook her head and gave a sort of rueful laugh. 'Not really. Not just that. It's because I…' She stopped, and in the orange glow of the street light he saw her bite her lip.

'Go on.'

'Nothing.' She turned to look out of the window, so all he could see was the sharp line of her cheekbone and the hollow beneath it. 'I've given him cause to worry in the past, that's all.

Poor old Miles is the one who has to bail me out and pick up the pieces.'

'What about your parents? Where are they?'

'My father's a diplomat. He's posted in Cairo at the moment, but my parents have always lived abroad. Because Miles is nine years older than me he's always taken on the role of looking after me.'

Olivier tapped a finger impatiently on the butter-soft leather upholstery. *Looking after her?* Was that what he called it? From what he'd seen, Miles was just one in a long line of arrogant bastards who treated his sister like a possession. Like an object, with no right to thoughts and feelings and opinions of her own.

Hatred rose in his throat, hot and acidic, and then the irony of his reaction reasserted itself.

Touché.

The car slowed and came to a halt in a line of traffic waiting to pull up in front of the gallery's Millbank entrance. As it moved forwards again, to swing across the road, the sudden motion threw Bella against Olivier for a moment, and he automatically put a hand out to steady her. He could feel her heat through the slippery silk of her dress. Lust tore through him, jagged and painful, like shrapnel.

He got out of the car as soon as it stopped, without waiting for Louis to open the door, but the moment he did so a volley of flashbulbs erupted around him. As always, he ignored them, but as he turned to help Bella from the car the look of startled uncertainty on her face sent an unexpected wave of protectiveness surging through him. Pulling her into his body, shielding her face with his hand as the cluster of paparazzi struggled to get a shot, he pushed through them. Her heart beat wildly against his own ribs as he guided her up the steps to the entrance.

Dieu, he thought with bitter self-mockery, he was really beginning to embrace the idea of himself in the role of hero rather too enthusiastically. He'd be trading the Bentley in for a suit of armour and a white charger next.

Once inside the echoing marble hallway, he let her go immediately, relinquishing her trembling, slender body with savage relief. There was no doubt at all that seducing her would be a pleasure, as well as an appropriate way of closing the circle, but he hadn't bargained on listening to her family problems first. He didn't want to get to *know* her, he thought derisively. That just added unnecessary shades of grey to an issue that was essentially black and white.

There were old debts to settle between their families. She would be part of the payment. It was as simple as that. Taking her, and then discarding her as if she was nothing…nobody…that would go a long way to evening out the score. It would be a transaction, like so many others he handled day in, day out. She wasn't a fellow victim of the Lawrences' self-seeking ruthlessness and prejudice, for pity's sake. She was one of them.

He had to remember that, and remember what they had done to his father, and take the opportunity so generously presented to him by the hand of fate. The only thing he expected to feel— would allow himself to feel—was satisfaction when it was all complete.

Hopefully on two levels.

Bella blinked dazedly in the bright light of the vast space. The evening had taken on a dream-like quality, and she felt disorientated and bewildered. Everything had moved very fast; one minute it seemed she had been handing round canapés to self-important public figures, and the next she had been hurtling away from the party—away from her home and her family—with a man who was almost a stranger.

A stranger who made her feel more herself than she ever had with the people who were supposed to know her best. She was filled with a sudden longing to be back in Olivier's arms, crushed against the hardness of his chest, but he was already striding away from her across the polished floor. She felt her gaze rest hungrily for a moment on his broad shoulders and narrow hips as she followed him into the high, echoing hall where the reception was taking place, then, with some effort, tore her eyes away and looked around.

The octagonal room was packed with people, ranging from elderly *grandes dames,* dripping with grimy heirloom diamonds, to *nouveau* celebrity patrons and aggressively fashionable artistic types. The scene looked like the society page of a glossy magazine brought magically to life, and her hands fluttered nervously at the sequinned hem of her dress. Black was the predominant colour, and she found herself thinking wistfully of the vintage Balenciaga dress, now covered in caviar and lying on her bedroom floor. Her Portobello market smock suddenly felt very bright, very short, and very flimsy.

Olivier was coming back from collecting a couple of glasses of champagne from the table by the door, seemingly oblivious to all the heads that turned in his direction. No wonder people stared, she thought helplessly, making an effort not to look at him as he handed her a glass. He was, quite simply, the most compelling man she had ever seen. The most good-looking too, though that was almost incidental. There was a brooding, focused, self-contained quality about him, which she had noticed yesterday in the auction room, and which seemed to set him apart from everyone else.

He wasn't a team player, she thought with a shudder.

Champagne bubbles burst on her tongue. In the crush of people, Olivier's closeness was ten times more exhilarating than the alcohol, and her skin still tingled and burned where he'd held her against him. She felt that beneath her dress her flesh would bear marks where she'd touched him.

She took another hasty sip of champagne, only this time her

hand was so unsteady that the glass clattered slightly against her teeth. And then his hand closed around it, around the glass, and it should have steadied her but it didn't. It drove her wild.

'OK?'

She nodded, smiling ruefully and feeling the colour seep along her cheeks. 'Spectacularly wrongly dressed, but never mind.'

His face didn't show a flicker of reaction. 'I disagree. You're perfectly dressed. You're far too fiery and beautiful to be hidden away in black, so hold your head up and smile.'

Bella couldn't look at him as shimmering rivulets of pleasure ran through her. *Fiery and beautiful.* It made her sound like the person she wanted to be.

She laughed. 'No way. I don't even have lipstick on.'

Just then someone behind her pushed past, knocking her forwards slightly so that the back of the hand in which he held his champagne glass brushed her breast. Instantly the pleasure sharpened to piercing desire.

'Look at me.'

His voice was husky, the French accent more pronounced than ever. Slowly she lifted her head. His face was so completely expressionless that he looked almost bored, but there was an intense glitter in the depths of his eyes. And then, with a languid intimacy that made her forget that they were in a room full of people, he lifted his hand to her face, pressing his thumb to her mouth, rubbing, massaging her lips as they parted beneath his touch.

By the time he let his hand fall to his side again she was breathless and flushed.

'There.' He almost smiled. 'You look like you're wearing lipstick now.'

'Thank you.' Bella felt as if she was opening, unfurling, blossoming in the heat of his exotic presence. Her mouth felt bee-stung and effortlessly sexy, and taking a sip of champagne from the narrow flute felt like an act of outrageous wantonness. She felt shimmering and incandescent.

Fiery and beautiful.

She smiled, letting the chilled champagne slide down her throat. 'Maybe we should look at the paintings now?'

Before she combusted with desire.

He gave a curt nod of assent. 'I take it you've been here before?' he said, putting a protective arm around her to guide her through the crowd.

'Of course. This is one of my favourite places, but I've never been here at night before.' She tipped her head back, looking up at the majestic dome above them and thinking of the silent rooms spreading out on all sides, the familiar paintings hanging in the darkness. 'It's different…'

'Different? How?'

Because I'm with you.

'More exciting.' Her eyes held his. 'More intimate.'

One dark brow quirked upwards a fraction. 'Intimate? With all these people here?'

'Because it's dark. Everything is more intimate in the dark.'

He moved through the crowd and she followed, unsteady on her glorious, insane skyscraper heels and her legs that felt as if they were made of marshmallow. At one point they nearly got separated as the groups of people shifted and moved together after he passed, but he didn't let go of her hand—gripping it more tightly and turning back, making a passage through the crowd for her. Eventually they reached the door to the long gallery. It was quieter in here, with only a few small groups of people viewing the paintings.

'I never asked,' Bella said slightly breathlessly, desperately trying to regain her sense of reality and rationalise away the persistent, distracting throb of her desire. 'What is the exhibition?'

'It's called "Five Hundred Years of Flesh",' he said, looking down at her with that cool, focused stare that seemed to strip her bare and make her shiver. 'It's an exhibition of the nude in art.'

Her eyes widened. Still with her hand in his, he drew her into the cavernous space and placed her so she was standing in front of him. For a moment she gazed silently around as the drowsy beat of longing quickened into something even sharper, more urgent. On all sides naked bodies reclined and stood—beckoning and inviting, aloof and superior, or simply bored. And behind her, close enough for her to sense his heat and feel the primitive pull of his maleness, stood Olivier.

He dipped his head and spoke in a husky whisper, his breath caressing her neck. 'Where would you like to start?'

The question, deliberately ambiguous, unleashed a tidal wave of hot, wanton need within her, and she let out a low sigh of surrender. He put his hand on the back of her neck, sliding his fingers into her hair, his thumb massaging the base of her skull as she squirmed helplessly, pinioned with longing.

'Here,' she said throatily, threading her fingers through his and leading him further down the gallery to one of the most famous nudes of all. Manet's *Olympia* reclined on a bed, gazing straight out at the onlooker. A beautifully embroidered shawl was crumpled beneath her, and she wore one delicate high-heeled slipper. Behind her a maid was showing her a blowsy bouquet of wrapped flowers, and a cat arched itself at her feet, but she was oblivious to both.

Bella smiled into Olivier's eyes. 'Why waste time on the apprentices when you can go straight to the master?'

'*Olympia.*' Olivier barely glanced at it. Instead his gaze followed his own fingers as they trailed down the inside of her arm. 'Why this one?'

'I like her.'

Lifting her hand, he nodded slowly. His face was as still as ever, the habitual creases between his dark brows giving him an air of extreme concentration that almost pushed her over the edge. Her rapid, ragged breathing was loud in the quiet gallery, but she was powerless to do anything about it.

He brought her palm up to his mouth. 'Tell me why,' he said thoughtfully, his lips brushing her skin. 'Tell me what you like about her.'

Bella had to force herself to bring her head up, to open her eyes and concentrate on the painting, and not the ripples of ecstasy that were running along the nerves of her arm and spreading downwards. Olympia's eyes met hers across the two metres and the hundred years that separated them, and she seemed to absolutely understand how Bella was feeling.

'She has great taste in accessories...' Bella murmured drowsily, uncurling her fingers and spreading out her hand as Olivier's lips brushed the hollow at the crook of her elbow. 'The bracelet, and those perfect shoes. I like it that she's wearing them in bed.'

Olivier lifted his head, and then looked down at Bella's feet in their shiny black shoes with the high, high heels. Her insteps seemed to arch themselves involuntarily as she imagined him touching them. 'One of them. She's only wearing one of them,' he said huskily. 'She seems to have lost the other one. But go on.'

Bella was finding it hard to breathe. 'I...love...the shawl...I can imagine how the silk must feel against her skin...'

She cupped her hand against his face, feeling the hardness of his jaw and the slight roughness of stubble beneath her tingling palm. 'Do you like her, Olivier?'

He smiled properly then: a slow curving of his beautiful, sulky mouth that conveyed neither joy nor amusement, but something more subtle. An acceptance of challenge, perhaps.

'Yes.'

'Why? What do you like about her?'

'She was a prostitute, a member of the lower class,' he said, taking a step backwards and positioning himself behind her.

Without being distracted by the movement of his mouth as he spoke, she picked up the faint trace of sardonic bitterness in his tone. 'The painting was so shocking not because of her body, but because of her status. She was too real. Too *common*. The critics were horrified by her because she made sex seem so simple.'

Bella started as his fingers brushed her neck.

'But I like that she's not afraid…' he said more softly, moving his fingertips lightly along her jaw. 'I like it that she knows how powerful she is. And…' Holding her chin, he gently pulled her face round so she was looking up at him. 'And I like that the expression in her eyes is exactly the same as yours is now.'

Her indrawn breath made a sharp hissing sound, like rain on hot stone, and then she twisted round, finding his mouth with hers. She was holding the lapels of his jacket, clutching and twisting at the thick silk as savage instinct took over. The kiss was hard and urgent, a crashing finale to the slow crescendo of the last hours. The images around the walls merged and spun in a blur of colour as Bella abandoned herself to the kind of all-consuming pleasure that a thousand years of visualizing white sandy beaches couldn't possibly suppress. He tasted of cold champagne, but infinitely more intoxicating, and he filled her head and her mouth and her whole body.

There was a noise at the entrance to the gallery: a burst of laughter and raised voices as more people came into the room. Olivier straightened up, his hands still holding her face as he looked over her shoulder. The next moment a woman with a press badge round her neck had appeared beside him.

'Monsieur Moreau? Please excuse me, but I wonder if you'd give me a few words for a piece I'm doing on the exhibition for the weekend papers?'

Dazed and breathless, Bella slid away, raking a hand through her hair, pushing it back from her hot forehead as she wandered along the wall of paintings.

She was hopeless. A completely lost cause. What had just happened there was categorical evidence that when will-power had been dished out she'd been daydreaming at the back of the class. The friction between her hot thighs as she walked was exquisite and agonizing, and at that moment she felt as if she could conquer the world. Ever since she had been too young to know anything about sex, Miles had made her feel it was something scary, something dangerous, and she'd come to associate desire with loss of control. But tonight she'd learned he was wrong.

She no longer felt afraid. She just felt *alive*. And for the first time since she'd woken up in the hospital she was ridiculously glad about that.

Turning her head, she looked back at the woman in the painting. Olivier was right. Her pose was demure, her face serene, but her eyes spoke of sex. Something shifted and settled inside Bella's head. It was like the feeling of remembering something that had been floating just out of reach. With Olivier's touch on her body she felt like Olympia—sexy and powerful and passionate. It felt good, not frightening or destructive.

She was aware of a sensation of release, a lightening of tension as she looked up to find Olivier. He was still talking to the woman reporter, his face very still, very controlled.

She wanted him.

She *wanted* him, and Miles and the therapist were wrong. There was nothing unstable or unhealthy about it—she glanced back at Olympia. It was a strength, not a weakness. It was about *taking control*, not losing it.

Out of the corner of her eye she was aware of another group of people coming along the row of paintings, talking loudly. Something about one of the voices drew her attention and she looked up.

Instantly she felt the blood drain from her face and the air rush from her lungs. Standing a few feet away from her, an expression of suppressed amusement on his face, as if he was trying not to laugh at some hilarious private joke, was Dan Nightingale.

Olivier's patience was running out now. 'A few questions' was rapidly turning into an in-depth interview, and he wasn't in the mood. He was damned good at compartmentalizing his life and focusing absolutely on the task in hand, so was extremely disconcerted to find himself answering questions on his collection of twentieth-century art while simultaneously imagining peeling off the red silk dress of the girl standing at the other end of the room.

Yesterday in the street he had written her off as a vapid posh girl, and that was exactly how she'd appeared earlier this evening as she handed round the canapés in that anonymous black dress.

Not now. In scarlet silk, her chilly aristocratic perfection was transformed into something warmer and infinitely more appealing. It brought out the passion he had glimpsed in her in the auction room and gave her an air of wild Bohemianism that was irresistible.

Or maybe that wasn't the dress. Maybe that was her—the real Bella Lawrence. The girl her stiff, conventional family was so desperate to suppress. She reminded him of a butterfly who had been squeezed tightly in someone's fist so that her beautiful, vibrant wings were crushed and torn. But who still wanted to fly.

'So, Monsieur Moreau—can you tell me about your latest acquisition?' the journalist asked with a girlish flutter of her eyelashes.

Olivier thoughts flickered to the painting he'd bought yesterday. The house at St Laurien, and the other, secret painting hidden beneath it. *La Dame de la Croix* could easily have taken its place here, amongst the works of masters.

Had things been different.

Tersely he said, 'I don't want to give details at the moment.'

The journalist nodded, her eyes sliding slyly in Bella's direction. 'How about the one over there? She's very pretty…'

His face hardening ominously, Olivier followed her gaze to where Bella was now talking to a man with tousled blond hair. He was dressed in the unofficial uniform of the perennial art student—appallingly cut black suit and open-necked black shirt.

Something needled Olivier about how he was standing in front of her, leaning over her, dominating the space around her in a way that was almost territorial.

'I have nothing more to say,' he growled at the journalist, and, giving her an almost imperceptible nod of dismissal, he strode past her and made his way towards Bella and the blond man.

On second glance, Olivier thought scathingly, he was hardly a man. He was a boy, a pretty blond boy, as flaky and insubstantial as a pop pin-up, though clearly Bella thought otherwise. The eyes that had looked at him so adoringly only minutes before were now gazing with similar rapt fascination into the face of this…*boy*.

Anger pierced him, sharp and sudden. He'd almost been taken in by her little-girl-lost routine. He and the rest of the male population, apparently, he thought acidly as he watched the blond boy reach out and tuck the dark silk of her hair neatly behind her ear in a gesture which was unmistakably intimate.

Olivier felt as if he'd been punched in the stomach. It wasn't just anger. No, at least there was something pure and energizing about anger. The emotion which knocked the air from his lungs and made him want to double up was darker and more sinister.

Jealousy.

He'd started the evening with one aim in mind, he reminded himself bitterly. To seduce her. That was what he'd set out to do, and he'd almost allowed some ridiculous, uncharacteristic and completely misplaced sense of chivalry and sentimentality to stand in his way.

He should be grateful to this upstart for showing him how foolish he was being before it was too late. Bella Lawrence wasn't the innocent she pretended to be, and the big bad brother thing was clearly something she played up, to bring out the macho, chest-beating instincts in the men she flirted with.

She was as clever as she was beautiful, and she had played him like a fool.

As he approached she looked up at him, and he saw nameless emotion blazing in her midnight eyes.

'Are you ready to go?' he asked with savage courtesy.

'Yes, please.' She came towards him without hesitation. At least she had the decency to look uncomfortable at being caught out flirting with another man, when her lips were still swollen from his own kisses. Affections that were so easily transferred were essentially worthless. He summoned a glacial smile. At least he could now enjoy what was on offer without guilt.

Bella just concentrated on putting one foot in front of the other and keeping herself upright as they walked through the gallery. But if it hadn't been for the steel band of Olivier's arm around her, she wasn't sure she could have made it. It was a relief to step out into the purple and gold London night, but in the time it took for her to take a deep lungful of air Olivier's car had appeared from nowhere and she was being firmly guided towards it.

She'd been right when she'd said he was a magician, she thought distractedly. He made things happen. Unlike her, who had things happen *to* her.

Against the throb of the expensive engine, she sank back into the seat and said quietly, 'I'm sorry.'

Her throat felt tight, as if there was something lodged at its base. Seeing Dan had been a shock—but mainly because it had hammered home to her in one swift, devastatingly accurate blow how flimsy her feelings for him had been. She'd been in love with the idea of him, that was all. He was nothing, she could see that with painful clarity now, but it only made what had happened as a consequence seem all the more pointless.

Looking out of the window, Olivier pulled his silk bow tie undone. He was utterly offhand. 'What for?'

For being such a fool five months ago.

She bit her lip. 'Sorry that *he* turned up. He was just someone I—I knew, at art college—'

Olivier cut her off abruptly. 'There's no need to explain.'

Bella felt herself shrink a little inside. Die a little. She had *wanted* to explain, but immediately she bundled the thought up and shoved it to the back of her mind again. It was all rather ironic: there was Miles, forking out a fortune for the best therapist in London, and Bella would rather stick needles under her finger-nails than confide anything remotely significant to her. Yet here, in the hushed comfort of the moving car, she was overwhelmed by the need to talk about it to this strong, remote stranger.

Clamping her teeth together, she looked out onto the lit-up city.

No. Better to bury it. To forget, even though there were times when the effort of denial was almost too much. It wore her down, all this pretending, all this repression of thoughts and feelings. It was a constant battle, but tonight she'd been free of it just for a little while. When Olivier had held her, and kissed her, nothing else had mattered. The grey fog inside had been burned away; she had forgotten to be afraid.

The headlights of a passing car illuminated his inscrutable face for a moment. Bella felt suddenly wrung out with longing for him, and for the blissful oblivion he had given her. She wanted to forget again.

Shyly she looked up at him from under her lashes, half ashamed of the strength of her desire. 'Where are we going?' she asked huskily.

Olivier turned his dark gaze on her. 'That all depends on what you want to do.'

It wasn't an entirely deceptive statement. He had already chosen the outcome of the evening—that was a given—but the lead-up to it was still open for her to influence in any way she liked.

In the sodium glow of the streetlights he watched her eyes widen and her ripe lips part. Was she still thinking of that other man, the one who had stood too close to her and touched her hair? he wondered cynically. Of course he had no way of knowing, but there was one sure-fire way of obliterating him from her mind if she was…

He picked up her hand from the seat beside him and laced his fingers through hers.

'Are you hungry?'

Mutely she shook her head, so her sleek, silky hair gleamed in the lights beyond the hushed interior of the car.

'Are you tired? Do you want to go home?'

The question was a formality; they both knew that. She was sitting up very straight, her thighs pressed together, the seat belt separating her firm, high breasts. Everything about her seemed to quiver with suppressed energy. She was like a taut string, waiting to be played.

'No,' she whispered, so quietly it was little more than a sigh.

But Olivier heard, and smiled. Leaning forward, he slid back the glass that separated them from the driver.

'Louis, the apartment, *s'il vous plaît.*'

CHAPTER FIVE

BELLA HAD never seen anything like Olivier's apartment.

Three of the walls were dark crimson, covered with startlingly modern canvases, and the fourth was made entirely of glass. Apart from a hugely oversized white sofa and tall, steel-legged bar-type chair by the window, the long room was virtually empty, giving no distraction from either the stunning art or the glittering view of London spread out below.

It also gave nothing away about the man who owned it. Bella had wanted to see past the sophisticated designer armour plating that Olivier wore to the man beneath, and this place told her nothing.

Going over to the window, she pressed her palms against it. She felt slightly dizzy and let out her breath in a slow, uneven exhalation that fogged the glass and momentarily reduced the sparkling lights to a dull shimmer. Olivier had come to stand behind her, and when the cloud of her breath dissolved again she could see the contours of his face reflected in the glass. She felt hollowed out with wanting him.

'It's quite a view,' she said hesitantly. 'You must never get bored with looking at it.'

'Wrong,' he said, very softly. 'I'm bored with looking at it now. I'd much rather look at you.'

His hands came to rest lightly on her hips, massaging her body gently through the slippery silk of her dress. She felt boneless, helpless, as her head fell forward, her burning cheek coming to rest against the cool glass. Moving upwards, his fingers found the buttons at the back of her dress, and a moment later it slid from her shoulders and pooled at her feet in a whisper of scarlet.

For a second she was aware of nothing but the ecstasy of air on her heated skin, and then the fact that she was pressed against a window and wearing nothing but the briefest black silk bra and lace pants filtered into her lust-drenched brain. But Olivier's fingers were tracing a delicate pattern of bliss down her spine, and though she opened her mouth to protest the words wouldn't seem to form.

'The window…people can see…'

'Shh…' He dipped his head to her shoulder so she felt the warmth of his breath on her quivering skin. 'Not without the lights on. We're too high up. No one can see you.' Taking hold of her shoulders, he turned her gently around so she was looking up into his perfect, impassive face. 'Except me.'

There was a low vibration of arousal in his voice which was completely at odds with the composure of his expression. It thrilled her. Unconsciously she raised both her hands to her head, clutching at her hair, sliding her fingers through it as she submitted to his smoky, appraising stare.

There was nowhere to hide from him, or from the savage force of the feelings he aroused in her, and in that moment she knew this was what she had been born for and that there was no point in fighting it any longer. She had unleashed the tornado within, and now she had to learn to ride the storm.

She felt her mouth blossom into a sensuous smile. 'You're sure?'

'Of course. I'm never anything but.' He slipped a finger beneath her bra strap. 'Take this off.'

His arrogance should have infuriated her, but it didn't. It was the most powerful aphrodisiac imaginable.

Without taking her eyes from his, she reached round and unhooked her bra, letting the straps fall down her shoulders. But before he had a chance to glimpse what it concealed she threw him a glance of pure wickedness from beneath her hair and turned round again, so she was facing the glass. Only then, with the artful grace of a practised stripper, did she stretch out her arms and toss the bra aside. Pressing her hands flat against the window, she flexed her shoulders and moved her feet, still in their shiny high heels, a little wider apart.

It felt indescribably delicious. Wicked, dangerous, exhilarating. London lay spread at her feet, silent and sparkling. She felt omnipotent.

Fiery and beautiful.

The sound Olivier made was somewhere between a moan and a sigh. Reflected in the glass, his face was a mask of inscrutability, but Bella caught the ferocious gleam of desire in his eyes and it nearly undid her. His fingers traced a path around the top of her tiny lace panties, dipping lightly beneath the elastic, then retreating and circling, unhurried.

A shiver of desperate need ran through her, so powerful it was like a foretaste of anticipated bliss. The movements which a moment ago had been artful and calculated were now completely instinctual. Arching her back, she felt her pelvis tilt helplessly back towards him as her breasts pressed against the chill glass windowpane. He grasped her bottom in his big, powerful hands, sliding his fingers beneath the flimsy lace of her pants and pulling them downwards in one swift movement.

Fluidly, confidently, as if she were performing a movement in some passionate dance, she stepped out of them on her high heels and spun round. She was spreadeagled against the glass, her arms out, her head thrown back, her hair partially covering her face. Her breath was coming in staccato gasps.

Her swollen lips formed one word.

'*Please...*'

Olivier could barely hold back a primitive hiss of triumph as elation exploded like fireworks in the darkness of his heart. She was ready to beg him. This was what he had waited for. What he had wanted.

But in that instant he knew it wasn't enough.

He wanted to possess her wholly. And, more than that, he wanted to take her to such delirious heights of ecstasy that she would never forget him.

In a single stride he had crossed the space between them and, placing his hands on the glass on either side of her head, brought his mouth down on hers. Her lips parted beneath his as her trembling fingers grasped at the buttons of his dress shirt, but the starched fabric was unyielding. He both heard and felt her snarl of frustration against his mouth as she pulled with increasing desperation, until the buttons were torn apart and her hands found his bare skin, moving outwards, pushing the crisp cotton back over his shoulders to expose as much of his chest as she could to her sensual, questing touch before moving down to his belt.

The strength of her passion and her lack of inhibition were completely unexpected, and shook him more than he wanted to admit. He found himself holding back, unable to risk touching her body because he knew that if he did his careful veneer of control would be shattered.

He couldn't let that happen. He wouldn't let her do that to him. He had to stay in command.

Reaching behind him, he grabbed the steel bar chair that he had used to prop the painting on earlier and pulled it roughly towards them. Clasping her narrow ribs, he hitched her up, so that her bottom was resting on the edge of the chair, her long legs in their shiny high heels still reaching the floor. She was breathing in a series of soft gasps that curled like caressing fingers around his taut nerves. Her hands travelled across his back, beneath his shirt, making trails of scorching want.

He had to keep himself distant.

Kneeling on the floor in front of her, he parted her legs gently and brushed the backs of his fingers up the long length of her quivering thighs.

She was so perfect it almost hurt him to touch her.

He gritted his teeth against the tide of sheer, annihilating lust that threatened to engulf him as his thumbs reached the moist darkness at the top of her thighs. Dipping his head he breathed in her delicate musky scent and let his tongue slowly, languorously explore her secret folds. Braced against the chair, she cried out in a high, pure sound of complete abandon, which was like a sledgehammer on his fragile shell of control.

'Now, Olivier,' she gasped. '*Please…*'

That was it. Holding back now was impossible. Olivier straightened up in front of her. Oblivious to the lights of the city sparkling before him, he focused only on her dazzling, desire-darkened eyes as he reached into his back pocket for the small foil packet he had placed there so calculatingly earlier. Swiftly, she took it from him, tearing it open with her teeth and sliding the condom onto him with fingers that shook with impatience. There was no time for him to undress properly, and he thrust into her with savage hunger as she arched towards him, wrapping her legs around him and letting her head fall back against the glass in wordless ecstasy.

She was amazing.

Astonishing.

His kept his hands flat on the window on either side of her head while she held his shoulders with her hands and gripped him tightly between her strong thighs. Her mouth was near his ear, and he could feel her breath against his neck, hear her moans of bliss.

And then suddenly she gave a wild gasp and her legs tightened around him. Without thinking he gathered her into his arms, cradling her naked, pliant and beautiful body against him, and unleashed his own climax.

He'd expected to feel triumph or exhilaration; some sense of victory.

The vicious self-loathing and despair that wrapped itself around his heart as he held her against him rocked him to the core.

'Thank you, oh, *thank you*.'

Exhausted, and high on unimagined bliss, Bella breathed the words into the warmth of his chest. Her voice sounded cracked and dry. And stupid, she thought distantly, keeping her head pressed against him. What a stupid, gauche thing to say. She hoped he hadn't heard.

'You have the most amazingly good manners,' he remarked tonelessly, disentangling her arms from around his neck. 'I don't think I've ever slept with anyone before who said please and thank you during sex. You were obviously brought up extremely well.'

He'd heard. Knickers.

Bella put her feet on the floor and wondered if her shaking legs would take her weight if she tried to stand. 'I was,' she said, hoping her voice didn't betray the desolation she felt at the sudden loss of contact with his body. 'I'm cursed with eternal respectability and politeness.'

He had his back towards her as she took a couple of tentative steps, rotating her hips and flexing her stiffened spine.

'Looking at you now, I find that hard to believe.'

The harsh note of mockery in his voice made her freeze inside. Her head shot up. He had turned and was leaning against the glass, looking at her, and apart from his unbuttoned shirt he showed no outward sign of what had just taken place. With the glittering city behind him he looked completely unruffled, completely in command. He was master of all he surveyed, whereas she…

She was naked, apart from a pair of skyscraper heels…

And somehow they only made her feel *more* naked.

She crossed her arms across her chest, appalled by the cold sarcasm of his tone. She'd hardly expected hearts and flowers and sincere declarations of undying love, but this…this *total* withdrawal was like being shown a glimpse of heaven and then having the door slammed in her face. Her dress was lying on the floor at his feet, and she was just trying to decide whether it would be less humiliating to ask him to pass it to her or to go and pick it up herself when he said blandly, 'What were you thanking me for, anyway?'

She shook her head in embarrassment. 'Nothing. Doesn't matter.' Moving towards him, she stooped quickly to get the dress and, clutching it against her, straightened up again. Before she could back away he had caught her around the waist with one hand.

'Tell me.'

His eyes bored into hers. There was no warmth in them, just a peculiar intensity that felt like despair. She looked down, struggling to think of some way of answering him that would sound light and amusing and casual, but the feel of his hand on her hip and the nearness of him scattered her thoughts like petals in the wind, so there was nothing left in her head but the truth.

The embarrassing, undeniable truth.

'I wanted to thank you for making me feel like that,' she said hoarsely. 'I didn't ever quite *get* it before, with…other boyfriends… I didn't know it could be like that. That…powerful.'

Her voice had dropped to a whisper, and she could feel the colour flaming in her cheeks. Abruptly he pulled his hand away, and she saw it clench into a fist as he brought it back to his side. His face was an emotionless mask.

Obviously the pleasure had been purely on her side.

He nodded curtly, then gave a brief, ironic smile. 'Any time. I'll get Louis to take you home.'

As she watched him pick up his jacket from where he'd

thrown it onto the huge white sofa and take his phone from the inside pocket, keeping the hurt from showing on her face was one of the hardest things Bella had ever done. She felt numb with shock, still anaesthetised by the after-effects of the violent pleasure that had just ripped through her, and it was only this that enabled her to summon a smile and hold her head high. Part of her was achingly bewildered by his sudden glacial detachment, but part of her understood completely.

She had sensed it at the gallery. Olivier Moreau was not a man who gave anything of himself to anyone. He was a lone wolf. The sex was spectacular, but intimacy was not part of the package.

How hideously humiliating that she'd behaved as if it was.

Louis was taking his time to answer. He clearly hadn't expected Olivier to require his services so soon. He wasn't the only one, thought Bella wretchedly, making her way to the door.

'Could you tell me where the bathroom is?'

Holding the phone against his ear, Olivier nodded vaguely in the direction of the corridor. 'Second on the left.'

With her dress still held around her, Bella tiptoed out and pulled the door closed behind her. Out in the corridor, she swiftly slipped the scarlet silk back over her head, smoothed a shaking hand over her hair, then took a deep breath.

A flickering pulse of anger had begun to beat unsteadily in her battered heart, and the insides of her wrists stung and burned. She rubbed them together.

Not again. She wasn't going there again. She was stronger now—more powerful. A sudden image of Olympia flashed into her mind's eye, and Bella recalled the serenity and the sense of quiet self-possession that exuded from her, making it perfectly clear that she was at the beck and call of no man.

Bella's high heels made no sound on the muffling thickness of the cream carpet as she walked quickly down the corridor and let herself out of the front door.

CHAPTER SIX

Normandy, France. One month later.

CELIA'S ancient MG sports car was—like its owner—eccentric, charming and totally unreliable. It had a fold-down hood in cracked black canvas that was remarkably difficult to work, a radio that only picked up two channels, and a throaty, spluttering cough that sounded like the death rattle of a lifelong smoker.

Bella adored it.

She had forgotten how much she also adored France. Leaving behind the industrial grimness of Le Havre, and rejecting the blandness of the autoroute, she chose instead the smaller roads that followed the meandering path of the Seine through the luscious heart of Normandy, and found herself in the middle of a Pre-Raphaelite landscape. Autumn was at its spectacular, flaming height, and the low sun lit everything in such a way as to make it look improbably lovely.

Fiery and beautiful.

The words materialised in her mind involuntarily, and she gritted her teeth and shifted up a gear.

That night in London just over a month ago had marked a turning point for her in many ways. Since then she had stopped trying to hide or deny out of existence negative thoughts or uncomfortable feelings. Not all of them anyway—just the ones centring on Olivier Moreau, which, admittedly, accounted for a fairly high percentage.

For as long as she could remember she had dealt with problems by retreating into a place inside her head where she was safe, and it felt as if Olivier had opened up that secret place and left her nowhere to hide. In the most blissful, brutal way possible he had forced her to feel again. Pleasure and pain, ecstasy and agony, heaven and hell. The aftermath had been difficult and humiliating and shocking, but those brief moments when she had stood naked and defiant before the entire city had done more for her fragile sense of self than a lifetime of stilted sessions with the expensive therapist could ever have achieved. Much to Miles's dismay she had cancelled her weekly appointments.

Maybe she just needed more sex, she mused sadly, gazing out over the lush Normandy countryside. But not with Olivier Moreau. With someone much more tender and romantic and human.

A wicked voice inside her broke crudely into her thoughts.

But just as skillful...

She came to a junction and slowed down to read the signpost, giving a groan of dismay as she discovered that Paris was still sixty kilometres away. The mellow afternoon sun was beginning to sink behind the glorious auburn fringe of beech trees on the horizon. She arched her aching back and was just wishing she hadn't decided to take the scenic route after all when she noticed the name on the signpost pointing in the opposite direction.

St Laurien.

It must be fate. Bella found herself turning not in the direction of Paris but off the main road and into a dense thicket of woodland, which cut out the mellow sunlight and plunged her into fragrant gloom. It was getting ridiculously late to be going on a nostalgic sightseeing tour, but she couldn't resist the temptation to have a quick look at the house where her grandmother had grown up. The house in the painting.

All of a sudden a dark shape hurtled out of the undergrowth at the side of the road. There was noise—a crashing of branches, a clattering of hooves—and Bella caught a fleeting, terrible glimpse of white rolling eyes and blood-red steaming nostrils as she pulled the steering wheel of the car around so hard it felt as if her arms were being yanked from their sockets. She came to a halt, skewed across the road.

Suddenly it was very quiet and very dark. Making a conscious effort to relax, trying to ease the iron bands of panic that had instantly closed around her chest, Bella took a couple of deep, deliberate breaths and unfastened her seatbelt.

It had been a horse. A riderless horse.

She got slowly out of the car and slammed the door. Her heart was thudding painfully against her ribs and she found she was very reluctant to leave the relative safety of the little red MG.

'Hello?'

Her voice echoed through the trees and dissolved into the thick gloom. She tried again. 'Hello? Is there anybody there?'

No one answered. But by that time she had already seen the body crumpled on the leaf-strewn ground.

For a moment she had a horrible certainty that the man was dead.

His face, lined with age, was an unearthly white, and blood from a cut on his forehead ran down into his silver-grey hair. But as she crouched down beside him his eyelids flickered and he made an attempt to sit up.

'Please don't move.' Gently she settled him back onto his bed of coppery leaves. 'You've had a fall. From your horse. I'm going to go back to my car and phone for help.'

Bella's heart was hammering against her ribs as she dialled for an ambulance, concentrating hard as she dredged up long-forgotten phrases from French lessons. When she got back to the man he was very still, and looked as if he was falling into deep sleep. She half remembered that was bad, and sat down beside him on the damp leaf-scented earth. He was wearing thick leather gloves, which seemed at odds with the warmth of the day, but she took his hand in his and held it tightly, willing him to stay with her.

Instinctively she started to speak, not bothered that he might not understand English, but more concerned with striking the right note of comforting optimism. 'So,' she began, her cheerful tone belying the anxious thud of her heart, 'you live nearby?'

He gave an almost imperceptible nod. *'Le Vieux Moulin…'*

The Old Mill. 'It sounds pretty,' she said enthusiastically, wincing at the banality of the comment but at the same time aware that it hardly mattered. This was life and death, not speed dating, and the important thing was to keep him conscious until help arrived, not dazzle him with her sparkling conversation. 'Do you have family?'

'Fils.'

'A son?' Excellent. She felt the weight of responsibility starting to slip from her and she squeezed his hand harder. 'If you give me his number I'll call him…'

The old man shook his head. The movement seemed to hurt him because his face was suddenly flooded with pain.

'Non. Non…'

'OK… Don't worry, please. It doesn't matter if you can't remember it. If you tell me his name I can find it.'

With great difficulty the old man opened his eyes. They were dark and troubled. *'Non*…please, you must not. He is very important…very successful…he must not be bothered because of me…'

Bella gave a small laugh. 'I'm sure he wouldn't like to hear you say that. You've had a bad fall. I'm sure he'd want to be with you.'

'No. He is busy…very busy. His job…very well paid. *Très important.* Please, you must not telephone. He will not come.'

'Shhh…' Bella soothed, holding both of his gloved hands in

hers reassuringly. 'OK, it's all right. Don't worry about that now. The ambulance will be here soon, and they'll get you to hospital where they can have a good look at you.'

It was as if she'd given him an electric shock. At the mention of the word hospital the man struggled to sit upright, his face contorting with agony. *'No! C'est impossible...* My horse, my home...I cannot leave. There is no one else to look after things...!'

Bella put her hands on his shoulders. They were broad, but even beneath the thick tweed of his jacket she could feel the sharp bones, and the dark eyes that fixed on her were filled with anguish that wrenched at her heart.

'Don't worry. Please, don't worry. I'll take care of everything.'

The words were out of her mouth before she'd had time to think. Instantly she felt the tension leave his frail body and he slumped backwards onto the ground, a look of relief on his paper-white face.

It was too late to backtrack now. Bella bit her lip and wondered what she'd let herself in for.

'So, she finally showed up.' Fabrice de Roche leaned back in his executive leather chair and let out a low breath of appreciation. 'I must say, Olivier, *mon ami,* there aren't too many women I'd wait fifty years to get a look at but this one's worth it. Genevieve Delacroix...what a beauty.' He tilted his head to one side, narrowing his eyes. 'Especially from this angle.'

One of Paris's top fine art dealers, Fabrice was a connoisseur of both women and paintings, but behind his insouciant charm beat the chilly heart of a businessman. His interest in *La Dame de la Croix* was professional as well as personal.

'Where did you find her?'

'A sale in London,' Olivier said tersely, and then, noticing Fabrice's look of surprise, added, 'Minor auction house, in a sale of French rustic junk. It was hidden under another canvas, an unsigned one. Something Julien painted after the fire.'

'Ah. So that's how it managed to disappear for so long. I wonder how it came to be on the market?'

Olivier gave a wintry smile. 'I assume he covered it up with the intention of protecting it. My mother was never very rational when it came to Genevieve Delacroix, and I imagine if she'd found it she would certainly have destroyed it. Unfortunately she also had a spiteful habit of giving anything he painted latterly to *brocantes* and *vide-greniers* just to emphasise to him how worthless it was, so probably that's what happened to this one. Who knows where it's been all this time?'

Fabrice nodded slowly, his dissipated blue eyes running over Genevieve Delacroix's elegant body. 'So, you need to know how much it's worth? I take it, as the other painting wasn't…ah…of the same standard, you picked it up for a song?'

'A thousand. Sterling.'

Once more Fabrice's face showed surprise. 'That's a lot for a minor work of…well, shall we just say "limited artistic merit".' Fabrice leaned forward, frowning slightly. 'Which suggests someone else was on to it.'

'How could they be? No one else knows for certain that it survived the fire.'

'Not for sure….' Fabrice let the words hang in the air for a moment before continuing. 'But you're well aware of the rumours about this painting. It's almost mythical. And let's just say that the Lawrence tribe have got fingers in a lot of pies.' Fabrice sat back again and inhaled deeply. A reformed forty-Gauloises-a-day man, his conversation was punctuated with pauses like this, as though the cigarettes had gone but the habit remained. 'With an election looming in Britain—in which Miles Lawrence with his very public views on morality and old-fashioned values is set to play a key role—they also have a lot to lose if this resurfaces now. Did you see who else was bidding for it?'

Olivier stood up abruptly and went to the window, which

wasn't perhaps a good idea. As he looked out across Paris as the autumn dusk fell, a vivid image of Bella Lawrence superimposed itself onto the glittering cityscape below…

'Yes.'

'Do you think it was someone connected with the Lawrences?'

…Bella Lawrence, beautiful and brazen, wearing nothing but a look of defiant invitation and a pair of high-heeled shoes.

'It was.'

Until now, uncertainty hadn't featured much in Olivier Moreau's emotional repertoire, but then neither had wanting something and knowing it was out of his reach. The night when he'd made love with Bella Lawrence had changed a lot of things.

Though, of course, 'made love' was completely the wrong term. He had had sex with her, thoroughly and ruthlessly. Passionately. In his head he heard her voice again as she stood in front of him, naked and glorious, and said that she'd never known sex could be so powerful. At the time he'd made some cutting response, but the truth was he'd felt it too.

He had wanted to touch her on some deep level, to brand her so she wouldn't forget him, and then he had wanted to drop her. But it turned out that *he* was the one who couldn't forget, and *he* was the one who had been left high and dry when she'd walked out so bloody unexpectedly.

Damn her.

Fabrice cleared his throat. 'In that case, my friend, I'd say they're onto it. May I suggest you double up on security and make sure you have watertight insurance? I take it that's why you want a valuation… You're not thinking of selling?

Olivier turned back to Fabrice. 'Not mine to sell,' he said shortly. 'It belongs to my father.'

'Shame. So, what do you intend to do with it?'

Olivier frowned. A muscle was flickering in his tense jaw. 'Veronique Lemercier's an ex-girlfriend of mine.'

'The journalist?' Fabrice gave a low whistle as he pulled a bottle of Armagnac and two glasses from a drawer. 'Bit of a viper, isn't she? If she takes up the story, within a few days Genevieve Delacroix will have more exposure than a Hollywood celebrity. In every way.' Smiling, he splashed generous measures into each glass and pushed one across the desk. Oblivious to Olivier's black gloom, he raised his glass.

'Nice work, Olivier. Revenge, as they say, is sweet.'

Sweet?

Fortunately at that moment Olivier's private mobile rang, and he took the call, leaving Fabrice with his simplistic preconceptions intact. Revenge might be sweet, but it sure as hell left a very bitter aftertaste.

It was completely dark by the time Bella found herself bumping the MG up the potholed drive to Le Vieux Moulin. The ambulance hadn't been able to find them, and she felt as if she'd waited hours, during which time the old man had drifted in and out of consciousness. Sometimes there had been minutes at a time where he'd been perfectly lucid, and at others he'd been so silent that Bella had had to check and check again that he was still breathing.

By the time the paramedics had arrived it had been dark, and he had been very weak. Bella had taken off her coat and wrapped it around him, but he'd still seemed frighteningly cold and very frail. Once she'd seen him safely into the ambulance, and reassured him that she would take care of everything, she had spent a terrifying and utterly fruitless time trudging through the forest in search of the missing horse, until it had become too dark to see properly and even the sound of her own breathing had been enough to scare the life out of her. When she had got back into the car to continue the search by road she had felt failure and guilt gnawing at her as keenly as the cold.

Driving now into an uneven cobbled courtyard, she saw a huge, oddly shaped building rising up in front of her. The dim headlamps of the MG showed a muddle of lime plaster and timber, mullioned windows and steeply sloping roofs. A light burned in one window, spilling pale gold beams onto the mossy cobblestones.

Bella left her bag in the car and tentatively crossed the yard to the house. Her whole body was stiff with exhaustion, and her heart was hammering painfully against her aching ribs.

Why on earth had she agreed to do this?

Because, she thought grimly, sliding the key into the lock and pushing open a heavy wooden door, *this man's son is too busy and successful to bother with him and he has no one else. Because he's alone and frightened, and I want to help him.*

The dim light from the open door to her right illuminated a room that looked like something from a period drama, or the inside of an old galleon. Gnarled timbers criss-crossed walls of lime-washed plaster that bulged alarmingly, and the air was damp and chill, scented with age-old woodsmoke and apples. Bella shut the door quietly and moved hesitantly forward, feeling a prickle of unease.

The house was very quiet, very still. As if it was waiting for her.

Hardly daring to breathe, she tiptoed to the doorway of the room from which the light was coming. It was the kitchen—long and low-ceilinged, warmed by an archaic iron cooking range which stood in an inglenook fireplace big enough to stand up in. Possibly there was a time when this kitchen would have been considered state-of-the-art, but that time certainly hadn't been within the last two centuries.

How could someone still live like this?

She exhaled a long, shaky sigh as she moved forward, trailing her fingers over the worn surface of the scarred pine table in the centre of the room. There was a painting hanging on the wall beyond the fireplace and, wrapping her arms around herself to ward off the chill of apprehension, she walked towards it. It reminded her of—

Suddenly she was grabbed from behind.

Sheer, suffocating terror annihilated every thought or sensation as an arm closed like a band of steel around her waist and she was pulled against a hard, lean body. A thousand half-formed images and ideas blurred in her stupefied brain, but none broke through the smothering blackness of fear. She opened her mouth to scream just as a hand clamped over it.

For a second she thrashed and kicked wildly, then felt herself being yanked roughly round so she was facing her assailant.

The scream of panic that had risen in her throat dried up and her racing heart performed an elaborate back-flip as she found herself looking not into the crazed glare of a serial killer, but into the dark eyes of Olivier Moreau.

CHAPTER SEVEN

FOR A moment she felt a terrible, compelling urge to collapse against his strong chest and cling to him, but then her adrenalin levels subsided and reality reasserted itself. Pushing herself violently away from him she shrank back, breathing raggedly and staring at him in horror.

'My God. It's *you*...'

His dark brows quirked upwards a fraction and his mouth twitched into the faintest of glacial smiles. 'God?' he drawled. 'I'm flattered.'

'Don't be,' she snapped, wrapping her arms around herself. 'I didn't mean it like that. What are you doing here?'

Through a haze of confusion and hostility she watched him cross the room and take a couple of glasses from the crowded old dresser. He was dressed in a dark city suit and an ice-white shirt which looked totally out of place in the rustic simplicity of the kitchen, but the assured precision of his movements told her he was on familiar ground. Though it was a million miles from the sterile sophistication of his London apartment, Bella sensed straight away that he belonged here.

When he spoke his voice was like sharpened icicles. 'I came to see my father. He's in hospital—as you've no doubt already heard. I assume you thought that while the house was empty—'

'*Your father?*'

It came out as an exhalation of disbelief and disgust. Contempt blazed from her dark blue eyes, and in that moment she looked every inch an aristocratic Delacroix.

The anger that had burned slowly inside Olivier since the night she'd run out on him was fanned into white-hot flame.

'Yes.' He spoke almost without moving his lips. '*My father.* Don't try to pretend you hadn't worked that out already.'

Slowly Bella raised her head and met his gaze.

'Yes,' she said slowly, struggling to make sense of the events of the last baffling hours. 'I suppose I should have done. When he said that his son was too busy…too *important* to bother with him… perhaps I should have worked out that he was referring to you. After all, there can't be many people who are that bloody *cold.*'

Olivier's eyes narrowed dangerously. 'It was you who found him?'

'Yes, of course,' she said distractedly, thrusting a hand through the raven's wing of hair that fell across her face. 'What else would I be doing here?'

'I think that's obvious,' he said bitterly, taking down a bottle of red wine from the rack on the dresser and studying the label. 'It's rather a convenient coincidence, wouldn't you agree?'

Bella gave a breathy exhalation of incredulous laughter. '*Convenient?* Are you *kidding*? I could be reclining in a hot bath in a Parisian hotel right now, but instead I have spent the entire afternoon in the middle of nowhere on some kind of impromptu Extreme Survival Exercise.' She shook her head in utter disbelief. 'I suppose a *thank you* would be too much to expect?'

Olivier looked at her steadily. His eyes gleamed. 'I wasn't as well brought up as you were.'

Heat exploded in Bella's cheeks. And her knickers. He was watching her carefully, and she knew that he was thinking of the same thing. Remembering the same words. Dropping his gaze, he uncorked the wine in one smooth, expert movement. 'Though,' he continued, with a languid smile, pouring it into two glasses, 'while we're on the subject, I would have expected you to know better than to leave without saying goodbye.'

Bella lifted her chin defiantly. 'I thought I'd spare you the bother of having to make polite conversation while we waited for Louis to bring the car.'

'I told you—I don't do polite.'

'Obviously not,' she snapped. 'You don't do human very well either. Tell me, if I cut you would I find blood in your veins, or ice?'

He held a glass to her and for a moment they both stared at the dark ruby glint of the liquid in the low light. 'I'm sure you'd like to test the theory,' he drawled.

'Don't tempt me.'

He gave her a chilly smile. 'And don't judge me. Maybe you would find ice. But maybe it's better that way.'

She took the glass and held it against her chest, so that the light shone through it and cast a blood-red shadow across her heart. 'I'm not sure your father would agree with that.'

He looked at her steadily, coldly. 'You know nothing about my father.'

Anger and indignation flashed in her eyes. 'I know that when he was frightened and in pain he didn't want to *bother* you! He could have been dying, but according to him you're too important, too successful to be inconvenienced with a little detail like that!'

Olivier shrugged. 'Well, the hospital decided otherwise,' he said offhandedly. 'They notified me when he was admitted and I left a meeting to get there.'

It was so easy to provoke her, he thought, watching with savage satisfaction as fury and indignation stained her cheeks a deep rose. All her emotions were so near the surface that as soon as you scratched her they came spilling out. She couldn't lie to save her life, he'd bank on it, but Fabrice's warning still rang in his ears. How much did she know about *La Dame de la Croix?*

'How *noble,*' she snapped, then stopped abruptly and pressed her fingers to her temples. When she dropped her hands a moment later Olivier saw that she had drawn that thick, muffling veil back around herself, and she was looking at him with the same dull eyes that had so exasperated him in the street that day, and at Genevieve Delacroix's party. It was some kind of defence mechanism, he could see now. The thought was oddly unsettling.

She gave a tiny, brittle smile. 'Look, you're here now, so there's no need for me to stay,' she said flatly. 'I promised your father I'd look after the house and try to find his horse, but since you've taken the trouble to show up, *you* can do it.'

She made to move past him to the door, but he caught her arm. 'Don't be ridiculous.'

'I'm sorry?' she said coolly. 'Is it ridiculous to expect you to do something for your own father?'

'I was referring to you leaving tonight. You're not going anywhere. But, just for the record, my relationship with my father is absolutely nothing to do with you.'

'Maybe not.' She hesitated, as if deciding whether to continue, and then said, 'I don't care that you treated me like some executive toy to be picked up and used for an evening's entertainment and then thrown away without a second thought. At a stretch, that *could* be seen as the behaviour of a typical arrogant, high-handed, chauvinistic, self-satisfied male. What does make me angry is that you seem to apply the same emotionless principle to your father. In my eyes that's utterly unforgivable.'

The room was suddenly very quiet and very still. The space between them seemed charged with some kind of invisible energy. It gleamed in the depths of Olivier's eyes and sounded a low, sinister note of warning in his voice when he spoke. *'Unforgivable?'*

'Yes.'

He smiled. A cruel, beautiful smile. 'You're quite an expert. Am I to assume that your family is perfect?'

'You know it's not.' The note of anguish in her voice was barely detectable. 'But at least I'm loyal to them.'

Tipping his head back, he crossed his arms and regarded her with lazy speculation. 'Oh, yes,' he said with quiet brutality. 'Very loyal and very obedient. And I'd say that was your biggest problem.'

She wanted to speak. Wanted to defend herself or disagree. But she couldn't. Her lips parted, she looked up into his narrowed, penetrating stare and the words melted on her tongue.

He had seen inside her.

For a long moment they simply gazed at each other, and then with a note of quiet triumph he said, 'Perhaps you'd like to go upstairs to your room. I'll bring your things in from the car.'

'I can manage,' she said dully.

'I don't think so. I don't want you to do another one of your famous disappearing acts.'

It was only when she'd left, when he'd heard her going up the creaking stairs, that Olivier realised his whole body was rigid with tension. For a moment he stood motionless as the irony of her words echoed round his head.

He had to grip the edge of the table to stop himself reaching out and hurling his glass across the room, watching the wine run down the wall like blood.

Bella slept fitfully, disturbed and tormented by the thought of Olivier's presence somewhere nearby in the creaking old house. Arriving in the dark last night, she'd got an impression of a sprawling building made up of odd angles and surprising corners, and in her muddled, fretful half dreams the timbered passageways and low doorways stretched out before her in a never-ending labyrinth as she tried to escape from him.

Or to find him.

Perhaps it was just as well she'd given up believing in fate. If she still did she might start to get paranoid. The horrible coincidence of being thrown back into the company of the man she had come here hoping to forget was altogether too cruel to contemplate.

She must have fallen into a deeper sleep around dawn, because the next thing she knew the light falling through the thin linen curtains was the thick honey-gold of morning. A sense of alarm that she had allowed herself to let her guard down propelled her out of bed immediately, and, still clumsy with sleep, she pushed her feet swiftly into her long boots, zipping them up over her pyjamas before hurrying downstairs.

The deserted kitchen was warm, and buttery sunlight sloped though the mullioned windows, casting intricate criss-cross patterns on the flagstoned floor. There was no sign of Olivier, though from the heat coming from the range Bella knew that he must have been up for a while.

The thought made her heart give an uneven thud.

She went to the back door and pushed it open. A rush of sharp, apple-scented autumn air curled around her, and she closed her eyes for a second and breathed it in, savouring its perfumed sweetness. In front of her lay a small garden surrounded by a low wall of crumbling yellowish stone. A brick path cut between neat beds filled with blowsy lettuces, canes of beans and raspberries, sprawling, spidery strawberry plants. Beyond this tamed square, lush fields unfurled like green velvet, glittering with dew.

She'd been completely wrong about this place when she'd dismissed it as primitive, she thought, picking a fat, crimson raspberry and feeling its juice explode in her mouth as she leant over the wall to look at the fields.

It was. But it was also utterly idyllic.

The light, the luxuriance of colours and textures, made it an artist's paradise, and there was an air of timeless tranquillity about it that soothed some clamour within her that she hadn't even been aware of until now. It was as if the place inside her head had been conjured into real life. The safe place to which she'd always retreated.

The field beyond the wall sloped down slightly to an untidy hedge, in the centre of which stood a tree. Even from some distance away she could see that its branches were laden with fruit, and, drawing closer through the wet grass, she found that they were fat purple plums. Many of them lay in the grass at her feet and she picked one up, stroking the bloom from the cool flesh with the palm of her hand, lifting it to her face to smell its honeyed perfume before taking a bite.

It was perfect—sweet and juicy, and far too good to be left rotting on the ground. She began to collect up more, discarding the ones that were old or soft, but there were still too many to carry. Clamping the first one between her teeth, she pulled up the front of her stretchy vest top and made an apron of it, and then, crouching on the ground, began loading the others into it.

Suddenly the indolent peace of the morning was shattered by a thundering noise that shook the ground and sent a dart of panic through her. Cradling the plums in the front of her T-shirt, she leapt to her feet.

A horse came over the hedge, so close that it was almost on top of her. For an appalling, heart-stopping moment the sky was blotted out by its massive dark forequarters above her, the dull gleam of polished leather and sweating flesh. She froze, not daring to move as the rider swerved at the last minute and the flailing hooves and flying stirrups missed her by inches. She was trembling violently with shock as the horse came to a sliding, shuddering standstill a small distance away. Before it had even stopped moving the rider leapt off.

Her heart, crashing against her ribs at three times its normal speed, plummeted as she recognised Olivier. As he strode towards her she could see that his habitually inscrutable face was now set in a pale mask of fury.

'Next time you feel suicidal may I suggest something less dramatic?' he said with lethal sweetness. 'Pills and alcohol, perhaps? A nice sharp razorblade? Anything that doesn't involve me, in fact.'

Bella felt the blood leach from her head. She looked at him in mute horror.

'I'm…I'm sorry,' she whispered through white lips.

Olivier scowled. 'Are you hurt?'

She gave a tiny shake of her head. Her eyes were dark pools of anguish, and she didn't seem to notice when several of the plums she was holding in the front of her T-shirt rolled out and fell to the floor. She looked as if she was about to pass out.

Instantly he was beside her, wrapping an arm around her waist to hold her up. His fingers dug into the exposed skin of her midriff beneath her outstretched top. He gritted his teeth against an unwelcome and wholly inappropriate rush of lust.

'Bella?'

She seemed to gather herself, and looked up at him.

'I'm fine. Sorry. Sorry. I was just…'

'It's OK,' he said roughly. For a moment they looked at each other as a gulf of unspoken history opened up between them. Olivier felt as if his chest was being crushed. Slowly, as if the movement hurt him, he raised his hand to her ashen cheek.

He'd barely touched her before he snatched his hand back again and spun round away from her, thrusting his fingers through his hair as he strode over to where the horse was grazing quietly. Swinging effortlessly back into the saddle, he looked down at her. Some of the colour had returned to her cheeks, but the eyes that looked up at him were huge and filled with hurt.

Remorse pierced him. Remorse and bitterness and anger and

longing. Viciously pulling the horse round, he kicked it forward and galloped across the field towards the stables.

For a man who had spent his whole life carefully erasing emotion, all of that was a lot to deal with.

CHAPTER EIGHT

BELLA was in the kitchen when he came in from the stables. Standing at the primitive old sink, rinsing the plums she'd collected, she had her back to him and her head bent. Her dark hair fell forward, hiding her face, but the syrupy morning sunlight fell on her slender arms, glinting off the beads of water on her skin.

Olivier swallowed and busied himself looking for coffee and the battered stove-top coffeepot his father had always used.

'Was that your father's horse? You found it?' Bella asked in a slightly shaky voice.

'*Oui*,' he said curtly. 'I phoned the neighbouring farms this morning. Duval next door found the horse in the field with his cows at milking time. He seems none the worse for yesterday's drama.'

'That's good.' She shot him a rueful glance from behind the shiny fall of her hair. 'What about today's drama?'

'No harm done.'

The words came out more harshly than he'd intended, and he silently cursed himself as he leaned over her to fill the pot with water. *No harm done*. To the horse, maybe, but it was more than could be said for him. The encounter had shaken him more than he cared to admit.

It wasn't just that she could have been hurt. No, what had

jolted him so badly was her reaction afterwards, when he'd confronted her. She had looked so...*broken* for a second. Completely crushed. And it had made him see her vulnerability and hate himself for what he'd tried to do to her.

What he'd done.

He didn't want to be reminded. He didn't want to care. He just wanted to settle the score once and for all and get on with the future, having slain the demons of the past.

On the marble shelf of the larder he found eggs, and went outside to look for tarragon and thyme. The sharp, astringent scent they released as he picked them made him feel suddenly inexpressibly lonely, taking him back to countless other haphazard, thrown-together meals when it had been just him and Julien. He breathed in, remembering the silence, the atmosphere of sadness and loss. Of suffering.

That was the look that he'd seen on Bella's face before.

He pictured her standing there, her eyes huge and dark in her bloodless face. Haunted, that was how she'd looked.

He pushed the thought away, sneering inwardly at his own sentimentality. *Haunted?* What he really meant was that she'd looked damned hot, standing there in her pyjamas and boots with her top lifted up and a deliciously enticing sweep of her midriff exposed. She'd looked sleepy and tousled and infinitely kissable, which was exactly what he'd almost done. *That* was what bothered him, if he was going to be brutally honest. Not anything to do with *her* being haunted, but the fact that *he* felt completely bloody possessed by the need to bed her.

Again. Oh, God, *again*, and it was nothing to do with revenge or the past and everything to do with her.

He remembered the first time he had set eyes on her in the auction house, how he had automatically singled her out because of her looks. Same old routine, he'd thought. A meaningless piece of flirtation like countless others with innumerable anonymous pretty girls who had slid from his memory the moment they were out of his sight and his bed.

But it was as if some wrathful feminist goddess had specifically thrown Bella Lawrence into his path as punishment for his hubris, his arrogance. The one woman in the world who, it turned out, could undermine his rock-solid self-assurance, tear down the elaborately constructed walls he'd built around himself and pluck cords of feeling that were beyond the reach of all the others.

He hated her for making it feel so good.

Bella took down two thick pottery mugs from the dresser and laid the table with greenish-glazed plates and old bone-handled knives and forks. They felt solid and heavy in her hands, and she ran her fingers appreciatively over the worn surface of a knife. Celia would go mad for these.

Olivier came in from the garden, his big hands full of herbs, his face grim. Going over to the range, he didn't even glance at her. He was wearing a pale blue shirt, unbuttoned over a white T-shirt, and, leaning against the sink, she couldn't help staring at the way the low sun brought out strands of deep gold that she'd never noticed before in his hair, turning it from dark brown to rich, burnished tortoiseshell. It curled just above the collar of the shirt, leaving a strip of tanned skin that, in spite of herself, her fingers itched to touch.

What was the matter with her this morning? Maybe it was the restless night, or her earlier brush with death, but she felt painfully conscious of her own body; the beat of her heart and the feeling of her clothes against her skin. She was horribly aware of Olivier's body too, and the way his presence seemed to fill every corner of the low, sunlit kitchen.

There was an effortless grace to his movements, she thought despairingly as she watched him stir the eggs in the pan, noticing how the muscles rippled and flexed beneath the butterscotch skin of his forearms. Whether he was dressed in an immaculate dinner jacket and drinking champagne at the Tate, or making breakfast here in this ancient kitchen, he carried the same aura of intense, focused power and sexuality.

He turned round and glanced at her as he slid a perfect herb omelette onto her plate, and she blushed, aware that he'd caught her staring at him.

'Thanks.' She sat down awkwardly and, picking up her fork, took a mouthful of omelette. It was so light it seemed to melt on her tongue. Olivier sat down opposite and she felt suddenly shy. The peaceful domesticity of the situation was deeply unsettling, especially in the face of his cold, brooding silence.

'So,' she said in a low, halting voice, needing to fill the silence, 'when was the last time you came back here?'

She thought she saw him tense for a second, but when he spoke his voice was completely emotionless.

'I left twelve years ago and I've never been back. Amazingly enough it's still exactly the same as the day I left,' he said, glancing derisively around the kitchen.

'Did you expect it to be different?'

'No.' His gaze came to rest on her, and she had the uncomfortable sensation that he was stripping her bare. 'Around here nothing has changed for centuries. That's exactly why I got out.'

Bella lifted her chin an inch. There was something challenging in the way he was looking at her that made her feel both uncomfortable and confused. She picked up the coffee pot and poured more of the dark, fragrant liquid into her mug. 'Some people might say that's a good thing. There's something reassuring about things staying the same.'

'That depends on your perspective. It must be very reassuring if you have the upper hand. If you're the one who calls the shots.'

He spoke with a quiet ferocity that sent a shiver down her spine.

'What do you mean?'

'Places like St Laurien are still essentially feudal. All the wealth and power is held by a tiny minority, which can cause…problems.' He skewered a piece of omelette with sharp precision.

'Envy? Resentment? The need to be the dominant alpha male?' she said flippantly. 'Those kind of problems?'

Instantly his face darkened ominously and she wished she could take the words back. 'I suppose you think that peasants should just know their place?'

'No!' The brutality in his voice shocked her into indignation and she got up, busying herself by clearing the table. 'You're twisting everything I say! I just think that families should stick together, that's all. You know, look after each other. Be there.'

'I see. Like your parents are there for you?'

Her hands, stacking the plates, stilled. She stood with her head bent as his soft, deceptively innocuous words sank in, finding their target right in the insecure, lonely heart of her. Biting her lip, she forced herself to pick up the plates and turn around to put them by the sink, grateful for the excuse to escape the intensity of his all-seeing gaze.

'That's different,' she said stiffly. 'My family has a wider responsibility—I've always accepted that. It's part of who they are and what they do.'

From behind her she heard his scornful gust of laughter. 'A *wider responsibility*?' he echoed derisively. 'You mean they're too busy looking after the rest of the world to bother with you?'

'Yes, I suppose you could put it like that.' She ran hot water into the sink. 'But that's OK. I don't mind. Their role—in politics and government—means they always put the greater good before their own personal interests.'

For a moment he didn't reply. She didn't turn round but was aware of him moving across the kitchen towards her. She could feel the hairs stand up on the back of her neck as he came close, and with exaggerated calm he leaned over her and dropped his mug into the water.

She glanced up then, and felt her mouth go dry as she met his eyes. The hostility and contempt in them chilled her.

'You really believe that?' he said scathingly.

'Yes, of course. It's who they are, what they were born to.'

She made a brave attempt to keep her voice cool and strong, which wasn't easy given that he was standing close enough for her to be able to see the flecks of gold glittering in his dark eyes and the tiny crease at the corner of his lush mouth. She looked sharply away, concentrating on the dishes in the sink, and then realised she was holding his cup in her hand, running her fingers along the place his lips had just touched.

Her hands stopped moving. Heat exploded inside her.

Mercifully he moved away then, shaking his head slowly as if in disbelief. Gradually she found she could breathe again and anger temporarily overcame desire.

'You might criticise,' she said through gritted teeth, 'but at least we stick together. You just *left* your father. You cut yourself off without a backward glance.'

'You're making a lot of assumptions,' he said acidly. 'I said I've never been back. I didn't say I cut myself off from him.'

'Right—so you clearly take really good care of him,' she said sarcastically, turning round to face him as her anger gained strength. 'You're what—a millionaire? And just look at this place.' She held up dripping hands. 'Not so much as a dishwasher.'

A dangerous stillness seemed to come over him. Leaning back with deceptive nonchalance against the fireplace, he crossed his arms and looked at her steadily, almost challengingly. 'Firstly, you considerably undervalue my worth. And secondly, this might not be my ideal home, but it is my father's. He *chooses* to live here. He won't leave.'

'OK,' she said with deliberate and exaggerated patience. 'I can see why he doesn't want to leave, because it's beautiful. Or could be. But would it kill you to make it more comfortable for him? To—I don't know—forgo the odd Picasso in favour of central heating and windows that fit?'

'Who says I'd have to forgo the Picasso? As you said, money isn't the issue.'

'I see.' His unwavering, laser-beam gaze was making Bella feel deeply flustered. Turning back to the sink, she spoke through lips that were stiff with hostility. 'So you could very easily help him out, but you won't.'

Suddenly the electric tension in the kitchen seemed as thick and palpable as the shafts of low sunlight slanting through the small windows. Bella waited, her heart hammering hard, and wondered if she'd gone too far.

'Oh, dear.' Slowly he levered himself away from the fireplace and came towards her. He sounded bored, but his eyes glittered with malice. 'If only life really was that simple.'

Pressed up against the sink, there was no means of escape. 'What do you mean?' she stammered.

'You still don't get it, do you? OK, I'll spell it out to you. The mill doesn't belong to my father. He's a *tenant*.' He enunciated the word very clearly, as if he was talking to a child. An extremely stupid child. Bella felt the pressure in her head rise a couple of notches.

'Well, couldn't you buy the house for him?'

He laughed bitterly. 'I've lost track of the number of times I've tried to buy this damp, rotting pile of timber—the last offer I made was twice as much as I'd just paid for the apartment on Park Lane. It's not for sale.'

He was right in front of her now. Bella looked down at the flagstoned floor, letting her hair fall like a firewall between them and waiting for the sick fluttering in her stomach, brought on by his nearness, to subside. But a moment later she felt a lightning bolt of electricity shoot through her as his fingers burned the side of her neck, smoothing her hair behind her ear, so he could look into her face. There was nowhere to hide from the hypnotic murmur of his voice. 'Trying to get improvements done is similarly unrewarding. The tenancy contract won't allow any alterations without permission. Funnily enough, it's always refused.'

White sandy beach. Blue skies. Tenancy agreements.

Taking a deep breath, Bella looked up at him and thought of Ashley. Poised, intelligent Ashley—what would she say in this situation?

'But that's not right,' she said shakily. 'Whoever owns the mill has a duty to keep it up to current standards. There must be… legal requirements. Surely the owners have no choice but to comply?'

There was a dangerous glitter in his eyes. Slowly, he reached out for the drawstring ribbon in her pyjama bottoms and pulled her gently towards him. 'You would think so, wouldn't you?'

Bella's breath quickened. He was looking at her with a mixture of amusement and something darker…more disturbing. More arousing.

'Then you have to do something…complain to the owners.'

'I am,' he said quietly. 'Right now. This property is part of the St Laurien estate, and as such is in the joint ownership of the Delacroix and Lawrence families. So, Mademoiselle Lawrence, perhaps you'd like to tell me what you're going to do about it?'

'There must be some mistake!' Bella whispered. Backed up against the sink, her whole body stiffened with shock. Olivier, by contrast, looked completely relaxed. There was something both insolent and sinister about the quiet drawl of his voice.

'Sadly not. Do you need to see evidence? Documents?'

'No, I don't mean that. I mean there must be some misunderstanding…about the maintenance of the property. My family would never…'

'What? Exploit their position? Abuse their power?'

She attempted a laugh. 'Don't be so overdramatic. They'd never deliberately force someone to live in substandard accommodation.' She was pleased with that. It sounded good—definitely the kind of thing Ashley would say. She managed a smile. 'Look, leave it to me. I'll go over to Le Manoir and see my uncle and I'm sure I'll be able to sort it out quite simply. Now, if you'll excuse me, I'll go and get dressed…'

On that note she stepped briskly past him, intending to sweep gracefully from the room. Unfortunately she'd forgotten that he was still holding onto the ribbon that held up her pyjama trousers, and as she moved she felt a pull as the bow came undone, and a sudden loosening at her waist.

With a gasp of indignation she turned round, snatching the ribbon from his fingers and tying it back up with shaking, savage fingers. But not before she knew he'd had a glimpse of her bare behind. His gaze flickered over her. The complete lack of interest on his dark, impassive face was more humiliating than anything.

'Good idea,' he said blandly, moving away from her to get more coffee. 'Be ready to leave in half an hour.'

She blinked in horror. 'You're not coming with me?'

'Not to see your uncle, no. Under the circumstances I hardly think that would be wise, but I need to go to the hospital to see my father, and since I got Louis to bring me from Paris last night I don't have a car.' He glanced up at her dismissively. 'You can give me a lift.'

As she'd spent the last half hour berating him for neglect, Bella could hardly argue, no matter how much she wanted to. With a stiff nod she left the room, cursing all the way upstairs.

She might not have been able to refuse to take him to the hospital, but she didn't have to make it easy either, Bella thought half an hour later as she went out to the car, carrying a basket of the

GET 2 BOOKS

We'd like to send you two *Harlequin Presents®* novels absolutely free. Accepting them puts you under no obligation to purchase any more books.

HOW TO GET YOUR 2 FREE BOOKS AND TWO FREE GIFTS

1. Return the reply card today, and we'll send you two *Harlequin Presents* novels, absolutely free! We'll even pay the postage!

2. Accepting free books places you under no obligation to buy anything, ever. Whatever you decide, the free books and gifts are yours to keep, free!

3. We hope that after receiving your free books you'll want to remain a subscriber, but the choice is yours—to continue or cancel, any time at all!

EXTRA BONUS

You'll also get two free mystery gifts! (worth about $10)

FREE!

Return this card promptly to get
2 FREE BOOKS and 2 FREE GIFTS!

HARLEQUIN® *Presents*

YES! Please send me 2 FREE *Harlequin Presents®* novels, and 2 free mystery gifts as well. I understand I am under no obligation to purchase anything, as explained on the back of this insert.

☐ I prefer the regular-print edition   ☐ I prefer the larger-print edition

306-HDL-EW7E   106-HDL-EXCQ   376-HDL-EW9F   176-HDL-EW9R

FIRST NAME   LAST NAME

ADDRESS

APT. #   CITY

STATE/PROV.   ZIP/POSTAL CODE

www.ReaderService.com

▶ DETACH AND MAIL CARD TODAY! ▼

(HX-P-05/09)

plums she had gathered that morning. The day was living up to its early promise, but although the low golden sun was deliciously warm, blue-black clouds had gathered behind it and the air was sharp. *So what?* she thought sulkily, wrestling with the hood on the MG. They might freeze, they might get soaked, but at least with the top down it would be noisy enough to make conversation impossible.

Olivier emerged from the house, unhurriedly checking his BlackBerry. Letting his gaze flicker casually to where Bella was waiting with ostentatious patience in the open-topped car, he stopped and said sardonically, 'You do realise how cold it's going to be driving with the top down?'

'It's fine,' Bella said stiffly. She had given her coat to Julien Moreau yesterday, but this morning, reluctantly aware of what Olivier had said to her that night at the Tate about wearing black, she had put aside her thickest sweater and jeans in favour of a short emerald-green velvet skirt with her boots, and a thin raspberry-pink wraparound cardigan. But he was right, of course. She was going to freeze. Putting down the hood of the car had been stupid, but she'd die of hypothermia before she let him see that. She cast him a supercilious smile.

'If you've quite finished fussing, can we go?'

The hospital to which Julien had been admitted was a modern building just outside Rouen, about twenty minutes' drive away. After a journey during which neither of them spoke, Bella dropped Olivier at the doorway.

She pulled up beneath a majestic sycamore tree and switched off the engine. He hadn't bothered taking the basket of plums in, she noticed resentfully, biting into one as she resigned herself to wait. He was right, it was damned cold, and holding the plum between her teeth for a moment she tucked her legs in their long boots up in front of her, wedging them against the steering wheel and wrapping her arms around them.

'Are you quite comfortable?'

She looked up with a start. Olivier was standing over her, watching her. She blushed and removed the plum from her mouth, hastily wiping away the juice that was running down her chin.

'That was quick. After twelve years you could only manage ten minutes?'

He opened the driver's door and took a step back. 'My father would like to meet you.'

The tone of his voice and the rigid set of his shoulders as he walked slightly ahead of her into the hospital left Bella in no doubt about what he thought about this. She followed him wordlessly up a long corridor, almost colliding with the solid wall of his body as he stopped outside a door and buzzed to gain admittance.

His face was like granite, the two frown lines between his brows more deeply carved than ever. For a second he hesitated, as if he wanted to speak, but then wearily he pulled open the door and gestured her through.

Julien Moreau lay against a bank of snowy pillows. His colour had returned, so that instead of yesterday's sickening pallor his skin was now a deep walnut-brown. His lined, weatherbeaten face broke into a slow, wide smile as he looked at Bella, and in that instant she caught a glimpse of what Olivier would look like if he relaxed. If he stopped being so angry.

'Mademoiselle…Lawrence. I have so much to thank you for.'

With a shy answering smile Bella stepped forward.

'Please, call me Bella.'

Julien laughed, though his eyes were filled with pain. 'Yes, I think that would be better.' And then he held out his hand.

She faltered, aware of Olivier's challenging, hostile gaze on her, focusing every ounce of her energy on keeping her smile in place as she took his hand in hers.

The skin was tight, paper-thin, puckered and stretched over

the bones. Raw, shiny, scarlet, it looked as if some time long ago the flesh had quite simply been melted away.

She held it gently, firmly, all the time smiling into his eyes. 'It's lovely to see you looking so much better,' she said softly. 'Everything at the mill is fine, and I brought you some of the windfalls from the plum tree. I hope you don't mind.'

Mistake.

Stupid, stupid mistake.

Striding back down the corridor half an hour later, Olivier thrust his clenched fists into the pockets of his jacket and quickened his pace.

He should have left her in the car. It was a mistake to make this personal. He felt like the watertight compartments of his life had been blown wide open.

Julien had been completely smitten, and the cruelty of that irony choked him. The space between himself and his father was so vast, so unbridgeable because of the devastation wrought on their family by the Lawrences...and yet *she* could come in here and touch the old man's shredded heart with just a smile.

Not that he could blame him. On Bella Lawrence's lips a smile could have roughly the same effect as a large measure of vintage cognac. He remembered again the moment when his father had held out one of his ravaged, ruined hands and Bella had taken it in her cool, pale and beautiful one.

He felt his own fingers flex as tension sizzled through every nerve. Tension and bitter, bitter resentment. Julien wouldn't have been so welcoming if he'd known that she was here to find his beloved painting and take it away from him again, he thought venomously.

The doors to the car park swept open and he took a deep lungful of cool air.

Bella slanted a shy glance up at him from behind her

curtain of dark hair. The tenderness in her eyes burned at his raw emotions like acid. 'Thank you for letting me come,' she said softly.

Her damned courtesy irritated him unreasonably. 'I didn't,' he drawled. 'You drove, remember? It was necessity, not generosity.'

'Letting me come in to meet your father, then.'

'Not my idea,' Olivier replied ungraciously. 'He asked.'

They were walking across the car park to where she'd left the battered red MG beneath the sycamore tree. As they approached a sharp gust of wind sent a flurry of gold and copper leaves spiralling from the tree, scattering them over the cracked leather seats like autumn confetti. Beside him, Bella shivered, and tugged the sleeves of her soft pink cardigan down over her hands.

'You didn't have to tell him I was here,' she said hesitantly. 'Or who I was. I thought that from what you said earlier he might not have…'

Olivier made a harsh, dismissive sound. 'Yes, well, it's amazing how far a bit of calculated feminine charm goes. Nicely done, Ms Lawrence. A flash of those big blue eyes, a flutter of those long lashes and fifty years of hostility and attrition are instantly blown away.'

There was a whooshing sound in Bella's ears. For a moment she stood perfectly still, staring incredulously at Olivier as adrenaline tingled and sizzled through her bloodstream and a crimson tide of fury washed her face.

'What did you *want* me to do, Olivier? Walk in there like the lady of the manor bestowing favour on a lowly peasant? She leaned towards him, the tense anger that had gripped her a moment ago suddenly giving way to an intoxicating languor. Dropping her voice to a low taunt, she tilted her face up to his and said softly, 'You'd actually *prefer* that, wouldn't you? You don't like being wrong about anything, and I guess you're used to people falling over themselves to please you and to be what you want them to be. Maybe I should just do you a favour and make your life easier by behaving like the *bitch* you think I am.'

And in one fluid movement she wrenched open the door of the MG and slipped into the driver's seat. For once the engine started first time, and she pressed her foot hard on the accelerator, firing it up in a roar of noise and exhaust fumes.

'Bella!'

He reached out for her but she yanked off the handbrake, shooting backwards out of his reach, and then, with a squeal of tyres, speeding forwards across the car park.

As the din of the throaty old engine died away in the distance Olivier was left standing there alone, rigid and speechless with fury. Until he'd met her, no woman had *ever* walked out on him, but now Bella Lawrence had done it twice.

There would not, he vowed, be a third time.

CHAPTER NINE

IT ONLY took a couple of minutes for Olivier to contact his PA in London and get her to arrange for a car for him. In a little under twenty minutes from the moment he had watched Bella storm out of the car park a sleek black Aston Martin appeared, with a far less exclusive car following behind it to take the delivery driver back to the hire company.

Showing not the slightest interest in the explanation of the car's high-tech computerised instrument panel and integral entertainment system, Olivier scrawled his signature across the form and got straight into the driver's seat, leaving the delivery man mouthing impotently as he drove off.

He drove fast, and with a terrible tense-jawed focus. Once out of the town he put his foot flat to the floor, sending the Aston Martin scorching through the lanes, whirlpools of leaves flying up in its wake.

The gates to Le Manoir St Laurien lay in a dip midway along a perfectly straight stretch of road, bordered on both sides by woodland. Speeding alongside the high stone wall that marked the boundary to the grand house, Olivier felt his hands tighten on the steering wheel as ahead of him the ornate iron gateway came into view.

And through it, a second later, the red MG.

It shot straight out into the road, barely pausing long enough to check that nothing was coming, and accelerated away in a billowing cloud of black exhaust fumes.

On the wrong side of the road. The English side.

Olivier let out a stream of vicious and extremely blue French.

The Aston Martin leapt forward with a roar as he slammed his foot down hard on the accelerator. The ancient MG was no match for it, but as he came up behind her he was horrified to glance down at his own speedometer and see just how fast she was going. Keeping his eyes fixed ahead, as if by watching her he could keep her safe, his fingers searched for the controls for the lights, or the horn, or anything he could use to get her attention, but the unfamiliar dashboard was designed for sleek minimalism rather than driving convenience and nothing came to hand.

Fury and frustration erupted inside him, tearing another succinct and colourful curse from his lips. Swerving to the right, he pulled alongside her, trying to catch her eye and order her to move over.

She saw him, of course. There was no way that she couldn't have. But stubbornly she kept her eyes fixed ahead. Her hair rippled out behind her, whipped by the wind, and her chin was lowered in determination. Against the steering wheel her knuckles showed pearl-white.

She was so preoccupied with their stupid fight that she was completely oblivious to the fact she was on the wrong side of the road.

His mind raced, fighting panic.

He accelerated the Aston Martin easily past her, then continued ahead of her on the correct side of the road, hoping that would make her realise her mistake, but in his rearview mirror he could see that her course hadn't altered. In front of him the road emerged from the cover of the trees and disappeared from view as it crested a hill.

Olivier thrust forwards and the needle on the Aston Martin's speedometer trembled. Reaching the top of the hill, he scanned the road ahead.

Dieu. Mon Dieu.

A farm truck was lumbering up the hill towards him, keeping steadfastly to its own side of the road… The side on which Bella was about to appear over the top of the hill behind him in that ridiculous, rusty death-trap of a car.

She wouldn't stand a chance.

He didn't have time to find the horn or flash the lights to warn the driver. Instantly, and without thinking, he swerved into the path of the oncoming truck, registering for a heart-stopping, slow-motion moment the driver's sudden expression of astonishment as he yanked the truck over to the other side of the road to avoid the idiot in the sports car. The two vehicles passed each other on the wrong side of the road, each of them missing each other by inches, at the same moment that the MG appeared over the crest of the hill, smoothly following the path of the Aston Martin.

The truck driver, recovering himself, sounded several loud furious blasts on the horn as he swerved back onto the correct side and drove on.

Heart pounding, blood thrumming in his ears, Olivier slowed down, swerving off the road and bringing the car to a standstill on a rutted and overgrown track into the woodland that sloped down to the river.

Bella pulled in behind him and watched him get out, slamming the door of the Aston Martin shut with such force that the car rocked on its suspension. Striding up to the MG, he wrenched the door open and grabbed her arm, pulling her roughly to her feet. The incandescent rage in his voice vibrated like an electrical charge in the mild, golden autumn afternoon.

'You could have been killed!'

'Like. You'd. *Care.*'

Held awkwardly against him, she spoke very quietly, enunciating each word with deadly precision. For a second his fingers tightened convulsively on her arms, and then he let her go so abruptly that she stumbled back against the side of the car. She'd never seen anyone look so angry. For the briefest second she thought he was going to hit her. Instead he thrust his splayed fingers through his hair in a gesture of barely controlled violence.

'If I didn't care,' he said in a low snarl, 'then why in hell's name would I have just risked my own neck for you?'

Bella folded her arms across her chest, as if trying to still the chaotic banging of her heart inside it. 'I don't know,' she spat, looking up at him with burning eyes. 'I really don't know why you'd do that, in view of the fact that you hate me so much.'

Clamping a hand over her mouth, she turned away from him and looked out over the fields. *Don't cry,* she told herself fiercely, and instantly felt a tide of rage rise up inside her like hot lava.

'I don't hate you.'

His words reached her as if from a great distance, barely penetrating the white noise in her head. Philippe Delacroix was as mad as a box of frogs, and the short time she had spent in the dilapidated, shadowy rooms of Le Manoir had been bizarre and frightening in equal measure, but, God, had she learned a lot.

Such as why her grandmother had been so understanding after what happened with Dan Nightingale.

Hugging herself tightly, as if that way she could keep herself together, Bella looked at the glowing trees and said as casually as possible, 'You didn't tell me that your father was an artist, Olivier.'

'I wonder why?' he said bitterly.

'Let me *think*—maybe because then I might have found out that he once painted a picture of my grandmother that was intended to ruin her reputation and bring down my entire family?'

Her voice rang with a mixture of triumph and despair. Olivier grasped her arm and spun her round, forcing her to face him. His fingers dug into her flesh and his eyes narrowed as they raked her face 'What did that bastard Delacroix tell you?'

Bella's hollow laugh was tinged with desolation. 'So you're not denying it, then?'

'The painting? Of course not—why would I deny it? You know as well as I do that it exists…' His words were ground out from between clenched teeth. 'After all, that's why you're here now, and it's what brought us together in the first place, isn't it?'

Bella stiffened and gave a ragged gasp of horror. '*What?* No! You're wrong! I…never knew. I thought…'

What had she thought? That it was fate, destiny…ridiculous romantic things like that that had made her path collide with the compelling man in the auction house? Oh, God. How could she have been so *stupid*?

Olivier's grip on her arm tightened. 'Don't tell me you didn't know about *La Dame de la Croix?* Don't tell me you weren't looking for it too?'

She seemed to try and shrink away from him, though he held her tightly. 'I'd never heard of it before now. And if I had I'd never have touched *you*,' she spat venomously. 'Because I know how it feels to be betrayed and exploited in the name of *art*. It happened to me too.'

He suddenly went very still. 'What do you mean?'

In the eyes that looked up into his Olivier saw a continent of desolation and hurt. 'Oh, yes. That's why I had to drop out of art school.' She took a shivery breath, steeling herself to continue. 'Not a painting, but photographs. *Naked* photographs of…of me, superimposed with newspaper headlines from way back when my grandfather was in the cabinet and made up into huge silkscreen prints.' Every word seemed to hurt her. 'Very modern…very clever—tapping so brilliantly into politics and the cult of celebrity, or something, but utterly *trashing* my dignity and my self-respect in the process.'

'Who did it?' he said hoarsely.

She tried to cover her face with her hands, but he was holding her wrists so tightly she ended up dropping her head almost onto his chest. 'The man I was talking to that night at the Tate. The man I thought I loved before I found out that he had only noticed me in the first place because of who I was. Because of my *name*.' She writhed and twisted in his iron grasp, trying to work herself free of his hands. 'That's why I know exactly how it feels to be stitched up and screwed over. I know how it feels to be on the receiving end of what your father did to my grandmother—'

'No!' His voice was like a gunshot in the still afternoon, and he pulled her against him, trying to stop her from thrashing around, trying to make her listen. 'It's not like that. The painting wasn't like that.'

This time she did break free, and sprang away from him, her eyes flashing with fury.

'Yeah, *right*,' she said with bitter sarcasm, and it was almost as if she was taunting him. 'Even though she was stark naked and wearing only the Delacroix cross—symbol of three hundred years of family honour—as a cheap pornographic prop. It was tasteful, I suppose. It was *art*.'

Olivier clenched his hands into fists and brought them up to his head. 'Yes,' he said in a voice that shook with rage. 'It *was*. It was…' He stopped, struggling to find the words in English or in French that would convey to her the tender sensuality…the *reverence* with which Julien had painted Genevieve. Immortalised her. Captured her and held her for ever as a beautiful, vibrant twenty-year-old with eyes full of passion…

Just like the girl in front of him.

Desire hit him like a punch, momentarily winding him. 'It was different. You have to believe me,' he almost gasped.

Her anger and bitterness seemed to have evaporated suddenly, leaving her looking just unbearably sad.

'How?' she said bleakly. 'How can I?'

He gave a low groan. 'You want me to show you?'

'Yes.'

He slammed her body against his as his mouth came down on hers, hard and relentlessly demanding. She felt herself go completely rigid as fury and frustration flooded every nerve and every cell, making her fingers grasp and twist at his clothes, her mouth open in a low, animal snarl as their teeth clashed and their tongues meshed.

And then suddenly she wasn't rigid any more, but arching against him; the fingers that tore and clawed did so now not from anger but from white-hot need. He was holding her face in both hands, his thumbs firm beneath her jaw, but then with a moan of what sounded like despair he dragged his lips from hers and tipped his head back, breathing hard.

Shocked, dazed with acute, agonizing desire and black confusion, Bella squeezed her eyes shut, resting her forehead against his chest and banging it gently against him.

And then, almost reluctantly, Olivier pulled away from her. His face was like stone.

'OK, then. I'll show you. I'll show you exactly what it was like. Come with me.'

CHAPTER TEN

NEITHER of them spoke as they walked along the overgrown track away from the cars. The low afternoon sun was as thick and golden as syrup, but it came from a sky that had darkened to a strange metallic purple colour, against which the turning leaves of the trees looked a surreal and beautiful acid-yellow.

Following Olivier through the wild undergrowth of bracken and brambles which pulled at her like tiny, grasping hands, Bella wanted to ask where they were going, but the words floated vaguely in her head and then dissolved again. Her heart thudded unevenly against her ribs, and she knew that it was nothing to do with trying to keep up with his pace and everything to do with what had just happened, what might happen next. She had no idea where he was taking her, only that her lips tingled and burned in the aftermath of his kiss, and her breasts felt swollen, ripe and tender.

They had only walked a little way when ahead of them, through the flaming trees, she saw a small stone building with boarded-up windows and a dilapidated roof of irregular slate tiles.

Reaching it, Olivier stopped and turned round. His face was tense, his jaw set, and the strange, other-worldly light painted a sheen of gold on his careless curls. The darkness in his eyes seemed to mirror the gathering blackness in the sky. As she caught up Bella realised they were right beside the river, and a little shingle beach led down from the doorway to the glassy green water.

'What is this place?'

Olivier stooped, turning over stones piled by the entrance until he found a key. 'It used to be a boathouse. My father used it as a studio.'

He stood back so she could go ahead of him into the gloom. Bella hesitated for a second, then stepped forward.

Inside it was velvet black, and smelled of moss and damp leaves. She shivered.

'But how could he paint here?' she said, trying to keep the tremor from her voice. 'It's so dark.'

A match flared, the sound making her start. For a second Olivier's face was illuminated by the bright leap of flame, and she felt her heart lurch as she saw the complete absence of emotion there. It was as hard and blank as stone.

He held the match to a candle, and then another and another, until soft light flickered tentatively into the corners of the room.

'It wasn't always. All around there used to be windows.'

He held the candle aloft so she could see. Bella let her gaze slide around the boarded-up spaces where light would once have spilled in, creating a perfect space to paint.

'What happened?' she said bleakly.

'There was a fire.'

'Here? Is that how he…?' Bella felt herself flinch as the image of Julien Moreau's scarred flesh came back to her. 'His hands?'

'Yes.'

Olivier moved away. His voice was a harsh rasp.

Broken glass crunched beneath the soles of Bella's boots as she took a few hesitant steps forward. At first glance the place looked completely derelict, but she noticed several indications that it was still used. There was a low bed or couch, covered by what looked like an old crimson velvet curtain, a wooden stool on which stood an empty wine bottle and a smeared glass, a damp-spotted mirror, and in the corner an easel, and a table scattered with brushes and tubes of paint.

Olivier was crouching in front of a small fireplace, coaxing a fire from a handful of dry wood, and Bella watched, transfixed as his big, capable hands hovered over the flames, shielding them from the draught, nurturing them until they took on an exuberant life of their own.

Like me, she thought. *Like he did to me the first time he kissed me.*

'Was this where he painted her?' she said in a low voice. 'My grandmother?'

'*Oui*. This was where he painted *La Dame de la Croix*.' Olivier straightened up and came to stand in front of her. 'It's one of his finest paintings. Most of the other up-and-coming portrait artists of the time were interested in pushing the boundaries, experimenting with texture and colour, and the results now seem quite…dated. Julien's approach was more in the tradition of Ingres or Courbet…more…luscious.'

Bella found herself mesmerised by his quiet, conversational tone, so that when his fingers found the tie of her cardigan and slowly pulled it undone she was unready. A small gasp escaped her.

He pulled back. 'Do you want me to show you how it was?' There was an edge of despair in his voice.

'Yes.'

'Then you have to trust me.' He hesitated for a heartbeat, and said bleakly. 'I *want* you to trust me.'

He was challenging her. She let her gaze move across his mouth, his beautiful mouth, and then looked slowly up into his eyes. They were fathomless pools in which her whole world seemed to spin. A dark chasm of need sucked at her and she knew she was lost.

'I trust you,' she whispered.

'Good.'

Time seemed to hitch and falter as he slid the cardigan off her shoulders. Longing shuddered through her, and she was aware of her fingers curling helplessly into fists. His eyes flickered downwards, over her shoulders, down across her breasts, while his exquisite face remained impassive. With one quick movement he unfastened her skirt, and it fell to the floor in a whisper of velvet. Then he turned away.

Bella didn't move.

He was standing by the easel with his back to her, his head bent. She remembered the painting in the gallery, Olympia on her silken bed with her level, knowing gaze. Heat throbbed and pulsed through her, and she waited.

He turned back towards her, and with a dart of piercing relief she saw the fierce blaze of desire in his eyes.

She made to move, aware that she was still wearing her underwear—tiny black lace knickers and a black bra, black hold-up stockings and her boots—but he said harshly, 'No.'

She stopped.

'Don't take anything more off.'

Olivier clenched his teeth. She was unreasonably beautiful. Looking at her was almost more than he could bear. If she undressed completely the self-control that was the foundation of his whole life would simply implode.

He needed to do this now. Needed to show her in a way that was more powerful than words what had happened all those years ago, and how wrongly Philippe Delacroix had presented it to her. The thought of him making it seem…meaningless, tawdry…crucified him. Bella deserved to know the truth.

Taking her fingers in his, touching her as little as possible, he led her to the velvet-covered couch and motioned for her to lie down.

Her eyes shimmered up at him, the desire in them naked and unashamed. Unquestioningly she settled herself on the couch, stretching out her long, long legs in their knee-high boots, drawing one knee up slightly, propping her head on her elbow. For a moment he gazed down at her body mutely, then crossed the small space to where the paints lay scattered on the table.

The image of Genevieve Lawrence in the painting rose up in front of him mockingly, her creamy skin brought to life beneath his father's sensuous brush, the jewelled cross lying warm and heavy on her naked breast. Quickly he squeezed smudges of thick watercolour onto a chipped china plate and picked up a jar of water, a long sable brush.

She made a small whimper as he stood over her, and he knew that it was the sound of raw longing. He knew it because he felt it too, but the darkness in the heart of him that had driven them for all these years dictated that he couldn't give in to it.

Not yet. There were too many ghosts crowding in the dark around them.

Frowning with concentration, he knelt in front of her. In the glow of the fire and the candles her pale skin shone like pearl. He registered the slight widening of her eyes as he dipped the brush in the water and tapped it against the side of the jar, but her gaze didn't waver.

As the sable brush touched the quivering skin on the slope of her neck she gave a small, shivering gasp. Olivier was aware of her tipping her head back, her fingers twisting in the red velvet as he bent over her, stroking the brush downwards over her collarbone, painting a ribbon of red onto her bare skin.

He didn't look up into her face, not trusting himself to resist the tormenting temptation of her ripe mouth, the open invitation in her lustrous eyes. Biting the insides of his cheeks to stop his focus from wandering, he kept his narrowed eyes fixed on the ivory silk of her skin and the image that blossomed there under the careful strokes of his brush.

The silence deepened, broken only by the soft gasp of her

breath. The fire was hot on his back as he worked, and at one point he threw down the brush, impatiently pulling his shirt from his belt and tearing open the buttons.

He heard her stifled moan.

It almost drove him over the edge, but he forced himself to go on, scowling now with the effort to keep the brush steady in his hand. Her chest was rising and falling hard, the creamy swell of her breast spilling over the black silk of her bra, and shivering beneath each caressing stroke of colour. The soft jasmine scent of her skin was almost unbearably enticing.

Focus. *Concentrate*.

In a small, writhing movement she shifted her legs, sliding one down over the other so the leather of her boots creaked quietly. He could feel a muscle in his jaw flickering with tension and savage, screaming want. He pushed the hair back from his face and plunged the brush into the water, wiping it impatiently on the trailing tails of his shirt before dipping it into the white paint. Nearly there. The movements his brush made now were gossamer touches, highlighting the jewel-bright hues.

At last he threw the brush down and got up, standing back to look down on her. A drowsy, languorous arousal lay over her like a veil. Her delicious, indolent beauty, now so reminiscent of the girl in the picture, was a knife in his side. He picked up the mirror that was propped against the wall behind the easel and, moving towards her, wordlessly held it up.

She lifted her head. Her eyes, opaque with desire, were almost hidden beneath the sweep of her dark lashes as she looked at what he had done.

'Ohh…'

It was a low, breathless exhalation of awe.

The candlelit reflection was of a goddess in a Renaissance painting. Lying back on the velvet couch, her head propped up on one hand, it seemed for all the world as if she wore a heavy, jewelled cross of gold and diamond and rubies on a crumpled length of crimson ribbon around her neck. It nestled between her breasts, resting slightly crookedly on the swell of her cleavage above her bra.

'So this is what it looks like?' she said haltingly.

Olivier nodded. He watched her exhale slowly and tip her head back, letting her liquid gaze linger hungrily on her own reflection. In that moment it was as if he had breathed life into the woman in the painting, and she was *La Dame de la Croix*— the mythical woman who had haunted and teased him and eluded him for so many years. He felt dizzy.

'Is it…exactly like this?' she asked softly.

'No.' His voice almost cracked. 'In the painting she wasn't wearing underwear.'

He wasn't looking at her, gazing instead into the depths of the shadows beyond her as he held out the mirror. Bella rose up from the couch in one sinuous, catlike movement and unhooked her bra, then slid her silk knickers down. The sound of her unzipping her boots stretched Olivier's last reserves of control to breaking point.

'Like this?'

She lay back on the bed again and looked up at him.

Slowly his gaze travelled over her.

'*La Dame de la Croix*,' he drawled quietly. 'Her hair was different…but otherwise you're very like her. Except for one thing…'

He put the mirror down and crossed the room to her. Bending down, he caught her chin between his fingers and captured her mouth with his, kissing her with all the pent-up fury and longing and frustration of the past hour and day and weeks. And then he tore his mouth away and stood back.

'Like that,' he said hoarsely, holding up the mirror for her again. 'Just like that.'

Heavy lidded, dazed, glittering, Bella's own reflected eyes looked back at her, and she knew that she had never felt more beautiful or more desirable. She was Olympia, but a thousand times more vibrant, a million times more sensual. She glowed with life and sex.

And suddenly, as if she were there, standing in the shadows and watching her own self, Genevieve's voice came back to her. *'Don't make the same mistake that I made.'*

Genevieve had loved the man who had painted her like that, and her family had made her give him up. The scattered pieces of the jigsaw slid into place.

'I see now how it was,' she said with quiet amazement. 'I *see*.'

Dazzled, she looked up into Olivier's face and saw the deep lines etched between his brows, the despair that gleamed in the depths of his eyes. The guttering candles cast deep shadows into the hollows of his cheeks and she reached out and stroked her fingers along one high cheekbone.

Gently, tenderly her lips brushed his cheek. His head fell back and she felt his low, hissing moan of anguish against her neck as he gathered her into his arms and pulled her roughly to his chest. Crushed against him, rocked by the urgency of his shuddering desire and unhinged by the strength of her own aching want, she fumbled with stiff fingers at his belt.

Triumph and annihilating despair mingled as Olivier gazed down on her luscious breasts, with the crumpled velvet ribbon holding the jewelled cross seeming to fall across them. He had got it right, he thought blackly. Just right.

His eyes met her blue Delacroix eyes, filled with hot, blatant need.

It was everything that he'd planned.

So why did he feel as if his heart had been torn out of him and thrown into the fire?

With sudden violence he seized her shoulders and covered

her mouth with his, and her instant leaping response was like fuel to the flames that consumed him. Swiftly she finished unbuttoning his jeans and pushed them roughly down over his hips so he felt the agonising relief of his aching arousal being freed from the confines of the unyielding fabric. He kicked them off. Her breath was hot against his ear, her hands grazed his waist, his midriff, and then finally closed around the pulsing heat of his erection.

He shouted his pleasure and his anguish into the muffling softness of her hair.

He could feel the throb and pulse of her silken body in his arms. Lying her down, he moved his hands down her ribs, across the quivering tautness of her stomach, then down... She bucked and gasped, and then went still and utterly silent as his fingers found the slippery heat beneath.

The world slowed and stretched. There was nothing but candlelight and bare skin and shuddering, shattering feeling. Heat exploded inside her under the delicate, insistent circling of his finger on what felt like the throbbing centre of her, and she felt as if he was touching her soul. The points of light made by the candles split into spiky, shimmering stars which seemed to ripple and sway as if they were lit beneath water.

And then they all seemed to converge into one dazzling ball of light, which gathered and pulsed and then split into a thousand glittering fragments as she felt herself shatter.

'Olivier...*now. Now.* I need you *now*... I can't wait any more. I *can't*...'

She was exquisite. Perfect. Helpless, engulfing need crashed through him as he folded her against his body and their hip bones clashed and ground together. Suddenly he wanted her cries of ecstasy to drown out the accusing voices in his head, the intense, focused urgency in her eyes to obliterate the ghosts of the past.

His mouth found hers and plundered it as they tumbled off

the low couch, pulling half of the velvet curtain with them. Holding her above him so he could see her face, Olivier pushed into her, hard, as he rolled onto the floor.

Pain ripped through him, sudden and shocking, as his bare back ground against the broken glass scattered on the wooden boards. Above him, wild and tousled and hopelessly beautiful, Bella writhed, her undulating hips sending screaming tremors of ecstasy through his body, so that they mingled with the searing agony of his tearing flesh.

Every thrust was torturous rapture.

His hands held her waist, and suddenly he felt her still beneath them. Then a violent shudder of bliss rocked her. Suddenly oblivious to the pain, he stopped fighting and gave himself up to glorious, thundering release. She fell forward, her hair caressing his face as she slid downwards and came to rest with her head on his chest.

The sweat cooled on their bodies as they both lay there, shuddering, gasping, shocked beyond words by the enormity of what had just happened. Gradually the frantic rhythm of their breathing slowed again, and she pressed her lips to his chest and murmured against the heated skin.

'I understand now. Thank you for making me see.'

She lifted her head and looked into his eyes for a moment before letting her head sink down again. Her voice was drowsy and infinitely soft.

'You were right. *La Dame de la Croix* isn't about hate. It never was. The picture was about love.'

CHAPTER ELEVEN

LOVE.

She was lying on top of him, her legs still straddling him, her hip bones still resting on his. Her cheek lay against his chest and beneath it he felt his heart seem to stop for a moment.

It was all about love.

Adrenalin rushed through him, and he sucked in a breath. He felt suddenly disorientated and light-headed. That was what he had wanted to make her see when he'd brought her down here, that was exactly what he'd been trying to prove, and yet he'd never actually *felt* that before. To him *La Dame de la Croix* was about power and tyranny, and since he'd had it in his possession he had not thought once about *love*.

He'd thought about revenge. That was the emotion that had brought him here, to this dark place with this girl with skin like velvet and eyes like midnight skies swimming with stars.

He had let himself become as bad as they were. As cold, as ruthless, as morally bankrupt. And the bitterest irony was that in doing so he had only proved them right. Fifty years ago the Delacroix family had thought that Julien Moreau was not good enough for their noble daughter, and that humiliation had driven Olivier to succeed.

And he had. Excessively.

But the cold, hard truth that had dawned on him just now was that he still wasn't good enough for Bella Lawrence, and he never would be.

She stirred. Raising herself up, she slid off his hips and came to rest beside him so she was looking into his face. Into him.

'You didn't tell me you were an artist too.'

'I'm not.' His voice was oddly flat, but Bella picked up a faint note of irony. 'I'm a city boy, remember?'

She pressed her lips against his warm skin and smiled. 'How could I forget? But the question is why a man with a talent like yours spends his life wearing a suit and sitting in boardrooms talking about money?'

She felt his muscles bunch and flex as he sat up stiffly. For the briefest second an expression of intense pain flickered across his face, but it was so quickly suppressed that she couldn't be sure she hadn't imagined it.

'If you knew how much I earned you wouldn't have to ask,' he said gruffly, moving so his back was against the couch, and reaching across for his shirt.

'Yes, I would,' she said quietly as the smile slowly faded from her face. 'Giving up what you care about—even if it is to earn millions—is like selling a bit of yourself.' Absently she caressed the painted cross with the tip of her finger, shivering slightly as she remembered the feel of his eyes on her, the whisper of his breath as he'd bent over her. 'You don't strike me as the kind of person to sell out, for any amount of money.'

Her words were like tiny darts that pierced his undefended heart. Wincing, Olivier got to his feet and bent to pick up the rest of their scattered clothes.

'I didn't "sell out". I decided to go into finance for a number of reasons.' He handed Bella her skirt without looking at her. 'Not just because I'm a shallow, emotionally bankrupt bastard.'

Still sitting on the floor, her legs tucked beneath her on the velvet curtain, Bella bit her lip. 'I'm sorry, Olivier. I shouldn't have said all that this morning.'

'Forget it. It doesn't matter.'

The terrible resignation in his voice sent shivers down her spine, but she couldn't leave it at that. She remembered the night of Genevieve's party, when he had danced with her in the quiet street and she had yearned to reach the man beneath the perfect mask. She recalled the sterile sophistication of his apartment and how, despite all that had happened between them there, she had felt more isolated from him than ever. Here, in this dark and broken place, she was seeing him. The *real* man behind the chilly self-assurance and the trappings of success.

She hesitated. 'Was your father disappointed that you didn't choose to pursue your art?'

'My father has no idea that I can even draw a straight line,' he said harshly.

Bella stopped in the middle of rolling one stocking up her leg. 'What do you mean?'

'I made sure he never knew. I never showed him anything I'd done. There was an art teacher at school who was very keen to encourage me, and found out all about fine art degree courses and wanted me to take exams, so in the end I just stopped going to lessons. I haven't painted anything since.' There was a matter-of-fact flatness to his voice, but as he did up his belt his hands moved sharply, viciously. 'Julien never knew I was remotely interested in art.'

Bella's throat was full of sand. 'Olivier, why?'

'Why do you think? He was a brilliant, talented artist, who in time would have undoubtedly become one of the geniuses of his generation. It was his whole life, and he lost it in the fire. How could I make him watch me achieve the things he never had a chance to?'

Bella stood up. Her heart was hammering painfully against

her chest as if it was trying to break out. Sudden, unexpected tears had gathered in her eyes and her face felt stiff with the effort of not letting them fall.

'So you channelled all your energy, all your brilliance, into making yourself a success in other ways, to make up for what you'd sacrificed for him?'

'Something like that.'

Olivier couldn't quite keep the bitterness from his voice, and he hated himself for it. Hated himself for having to lie to her, but the truth was too cruel. He'd channelled his energy into making himself a success to prove to *her* family that he was someone. To make himself every bit as powerful and wealthy as they were. To make sure that one day he could make them pay for what they'd done.

And now that time had come.

'Tell me about the fire,' she prompted softly.

Olivier felt his mouth go dry, and for a moment squeezed his eyes shut as her words seemed to hang in front of him, taunting and teasing.

Go on... Tell her, a voice inside him mocked. *Tell her about how it was started deliberately by Philippe Delacroix, that it was her own flesh and blood that knowingly, cold-bloodedly stripped Julien Moreau of everything. That's what you've wanted all this time, isn't it? To confront them with what they did?*

'There's nothing to tell,' he said harshly. 'It happened before I was born. Julien had been working for a huge exhibition in Paris's most prestigious gallery, and all his work was lost.'

'And his hands were so damaged he couldn't work again...?'

Olivier braced himself against the gentle compassion in her voice, but it seemed to curl itself around him, caressing him. He was powerless to resist.

'Yes. He went in, you see. He went in to get the only painting that mattered.' *The one painting that Philippe had wanted to destroy.*

'La Dame de la Croix.'

'Yes.'

Silently Bella came up behind him, sliding her arms around his waist and laying her cheek between his shoulders. Before he could bite it back, a low, sharp hiss of pain escaped him.

She stood back, her arms falling to her sides. When she spoke, the hurt in her voice made the pain in his back fade into insignificance.

'What's wrong?'

Slowly he shook his head. 'Nothing. Nothing's wrong.'

There was a certain poetry in it, he thought blackly. A pleasing symmetry and justice. He had set out with the intention of seducing her, of sleeping with her, purely to hurt her. That was what he had wanted the first time, back in London. Now his own pain was his punishment for that.

He was almost glad of it.

Outside it was raining.

The sky was a dark pewter colour, but the strange yellow light from the low sun persisted, and a lurid rainbow soared over the trees. The rain had stripped the branches further so they seemed to shiver in the half-light, and the broken surface of the river was choked with yellowing leaves.

Bella blinked and tipped her head back, letting the rain fall onto her flushed cheeks. After so long in secret darkness, suspended from the realities of time, it seemed bizarre that it should still be daylight, and she felt as she'd used to when she was a teenager, emerging into the noise and commotion of the street after two blissful hours of romantic fantasy in the dark of the cinema.

How she'd adored the cinema. It had been a legitimate outlet for all of the wild, passionate emotions that were so forbidden by the Lawrences. But now, stumbling out into the unearthly afternoon light and taking in a lungful of cool autumn air, she felt almost free of those bonds.

Olivier slid a hand around her neck, hooking her towards him, and her stomach tightened in a spasm of remembered pleasure. Getting dressed, putting on the armour of their clothes had created a little distance between them again, but a shiver rippled along the length of her spine as she thought of his body beneath them.

For all these years she had put herself last, swallowing the family line about duty and obedience, unquestioningly sacrificing her own freedom in order that nothing should cloud the mirror-shiny surface of the Lawrence–Delacroix family honour. She'd been a good girl for a long time, and now she was taking her reward.

And anyway, from this distance her family didn't seem so powerful or so frightening. Philippe Delacroix had been so twisted and embittered when he'd spoken of Julien Moreau, to the point where he had seemed pathetic, shut up all alone in that big empty museum of a house, still obsessed with events which were nothing but history.

She pitied him.

In fact, as Olivier gathered her into the shelter of his body, looking down at her with that inscrutable, appraising expression which drove her wild, she pitied anyone who wasn't her. And that, she realised, was a complete reversal of her normal outlook on life. All at once she was glad to be herself, rather than feeling the need to apologise for it.

'You have your top on inside out,' Olivier murmured gravely, close to her ear.

She felt a smile spread across her mouth as the heat spread downwards through her body. 'Who cares? I'm going to take it off again as soon as we get back to the house.'

'Is that a promise?'

Heat flared in his dark, faintly shadowed eyes and the smile died on her lips. Slowly, she ran her tongue over them, taking a step or two backwards and gazing up at him in unconcealed desire. His hair was dark with rain, one curl falling across his tanned forehead, and he brushed it back with his hand, momentarily compressing his lips against the rain that was running down his beautiful face.

Her senses kicked into overdrive.

This was what Miles and the expensive therapist had cautioned against. This wild, dizzying rush of joy and panic… But Bella knew it was what she had been born for. What she had been unconsciously craving all her life. Again Genevieve's words came back to her, and she knew that her grandmother had been right.

You have talent for loving…for giving…

There was so much she was just beginning to understand. She looked up into Olivier's face. The surreal acid-yellow light highlighted the two deep creases etched between his brows, and she brought her fingers up to his face, cupping her palm against his cheek.

'I've learned a lot this afternoon,' she said softly. 'You've helped me make sense of some of it.'

Painfully he shrugged off his coat, and gave her a crooked smile. 'It was my pleasure.'

He wrapped the coat around her, holding it firmly beneath her chin, and pulled her towards him. For a second he held her close against the shelter of his chest as he pressed his lips to her wet forehead. 'I've learned some things too…'

She sprang backwards suddenly, clamping her hand across her mouth and looking up at him in wide-eyed horror, and for a sickening moment he wondered if she'd guessed what he'd been thinking.

'Oh, no,' she wailed. 'Oh, God…'

Olivier's blood ran cold. 'What is it?'

Bella was already running ahead of him, clutching his coat around her, but as she ran she called back over her shoulder. 'The car! Celia's car! I left the top down!'

Olivier let his head roll back in relief. The car was easily put right. He'd replace it if necessary. Everything else was going to take a bit more unravelling.

Feeling his torn shoulders stinging as the rain soaked his shirt, he followed her thoughtfully, stopping to pick some huge, dark-gilled mushrooms from the base of a tree. He could see her up ahead, leaning into the car, her endless legs in their high boots the only part of her that was visible. His stomach flipped.

Dieu, but she was gorgeous. Vibrant and sexy and beautiful, with no trace left of the chilly dullness that she had worn like a shroud that first day in London. As he approached she was just getting gingerly into the soaking driver's seat. Starting up the wheezing, spluttering engine, she looked up at him with a smile that spread through his body like wildfire.

'Just when I thought my pants couldn't get any wetter…'

He'd vowed not to let her leave him a third time, and yet as he stood there and watched her drive off he felt no anger.

This time it was much more complicated.

Bella couldn't remember anything about the short drive back to the mill, apart from the tingling awareness of Olivier in the car behind her. Her body felt hollowed out, purged, blessed—as if she'd been through some elemental ritual or some baptismal fire and emerged cleaner, brighter, better.

Alive again.

She was herself. Maybe for the first time ever. She was simply a girl with a passion for life and a talent for love. And she was *proud* of that.

She glanced into the small rearview mirror of the MG and caught a glimpse of Olivier's face through the windscreen of the

Aston Martin behind her. It was utterly blank, completely inscrutable, but she felt fireworks of joy explode inside her. She
understood him now. Beneath the mask, beneath the expensive
suits, the beautiful shirts, she had seen the real man.

'Come on.'

With a little start of surprise she realised that they were back
at the mill, and that she had automatically stopped the car and
was sitting, lost in thought, with the engine still running. Olivier
leaned down and turned the ignition off, then opened the door
and held out his hand.

She took it and got up hesitantly. Her skirt was sodden from
the puddle of rainwater on the seat, and it stuck to her thighs.

Olivier raised an eyebrow. 'You're wet.'

Bella felt her breath catch in her throat. 'Yes,' she murmured,
as a smile blossomed on her lips. 'Very. I have to get dried off.'

Slowly, without smiling, he shook his head. 'Don't bother.'

Rain was dripping from the ends of her hair, running down
inside the turned-up collar of the coat he had wrapped around
her. It cloaked her in warmth and in his exquisite, unique scent.
The scent of his skin. Of him.

She felt her insides tremble.

'You're right,' she said huskily. 'No point.'

For a long moment they gazed at each other, and then wordlessly
he scooped her up into his arms and carried her into the house.

He shouldered open the door to the bedroom at the top of the
stairs and set her gently on her feet. Her skin flamed and fizzed,
hot and wet. She staggered very slightly as her knees refused to
take her own weight, and reached up to hold his shoulders as she
tilted her face up to kiss him. As she did so she saw him wince,
and pulled back.

'Get undressed,' he said hoarsely, stepping backwards. His
eyes were coal-black and impossible to read.

'Where are you going?'

'To run a bath.'

Left alone, Bella peeled the wet clothes off her hungry body and stood naked in the centre of the room. Her skin felt paper-thin, burning and glowing—like beaten gold.

Fiery and beautiful.

He had seen those qualities in her, even when she herself hadn't known they were there. Or maybe she had known, but had been ashamed of them. Hazily she looked up, catching sight of her own reflection in the fly-blown glass of the old dressing table mirror. Even in its murky depths the painted Delacroix cross seemed to gleam. Her eyes had a hectic, ravenous glitter and her lips were ruby dark. Engorged, like her other secret self…

Olivier appeared behind her. Their gazes locked.

She watched him place his hands on her shoulders, feeling waves of fresh heat ripple and billow through her at his touch. His thumbs massaged the base of her neck in lazy circles and a drop of rainwater fell from her sleek, wet hair and ran down her collar-bone, making the red of the painted ribbon run down, like blood.

Bella took a tiny, shivering inward breath.

'It's so perfect,' she murmured raggedly. 'I can't bear to spoil it.'

In the mirror she watched his eyes move slowly down over her quivering body with that deadpan detachment which made her heart race and liquid warmth flood into her pelvis. As they came back up to her face she caught the spark in their depths. 'Then allow me…'

He parted his lips and sucked the ball of his thumb before cupping her breast in the palm of his hand and sweeping his thumb across the jewelled cross, smudging the paint into a muddied streak.

She gasped.

'It's part of the past,' he said harshly.

In one fluid movement she was back in his arms, and he was carrying her along the corridor to the bathroom.

The high ceiling and grey-green walls of the large room were lost in swirling clouds of steam which curled around them, warm and languid, creating a secret world of blurred edges and dissolving colours. The sky beyond the frosted windows had darkened to a smoky blue, and the room was softly lit by an ancient, glass-shaded brass sconce on the wall, around which the steam made a halo of gold.

On the windowsill was a bottle of Muscadet, cool and green and moisture-beaded, and two glasses. Bella smiled. 'You think of everything.'

'Get in.'

She shook her head. 'Uh-uh. Not without you.'

Her hands went to the buttons of his paint-stained shirt, and with great concentration she began to undo them. Olivier stood, rock-like and motionless, his face stony as she gradually revealed the tanned expanse of his chest. When she reached the last one, she tugged the shirt free of his trousers and slipped it off his shoulders.

An expression of extreme suffering flickered across his face. It lasted no more than a fraction of a second, but Bella saw it before he could hide it behind his habitual inscrutable mask.

'Olivier?' she whispered.

He didn't move, didn't speak. Slowly, trailing her fingers across his hard chest she moved round so she was standing behind him.

The sound she made was somewhere between a groan and a sigh.

'My God. *My God*, Olivier.'

His shoulders were broad and phenomenally strong, tapering down to narrow hips, but the tanned skin was a mess of shallow cuts and drying blood.

Reverently she brushed her fingertips over them, remembering in a flash of anguished insight the crunch of glass beneath her boots as she crossed the boathouse floor.

'The glass—why didn't you say?'

Beneath her fingers she felt his muscles flex as he raised his shoulders in a small shrug.

'Stopping would have been much more painful,' he said hoarsely.

Bella felt raw with tenderness and ripe with longing. Her nipples, just inches from Olivier's back, stiffened and throbbed, and slick heat drenched her from within. She pressed her swollen lips to the torn skin and slid her arms around his waist. Still he did not move.

But as her fingers skimmed across his flat stomach she felt the muscles quiver and tighten, and just inching downwards a little she met the hard thrust of his erection.

A tremor ricocheted through his tense body.

It was all she needed to tip her over the edge of control. Without thinking, she found her hands were on the buckle of his belt, fumbling blindly with it as her mouth caressed and licked and explored the hard width of his shoulders. His hands were on hers, doing with ruthless efficiency what she was too dazed with desire to do properly, and the next thing she knew he had turned round and was scooping her into his arms as his lips came down on hers in a deep, devouring kiss.

He set her down gently in the steaming water, and got in behind her. In a delicious torpor of lust Bella slid down into the heat, and, tipping her head back, found his mouth again, darting out her tongue and caressing his lips in the lightest, the most promising of kisses. Lying against him, she could feel the hardness of his erection pressing into the small of her back, and for delicious moments arched herself against it, savouring the anticipation of feeling him inside her. Then lithely she flipped herself over and slipped beneath the water.

The clear greenish world she found herself in echoed with the throbbing of blood in her ears. His hard flesh felt almost cool in the heat of the water as she let her lips close over him, and ecstasy flooded her.

Long moments later she broke the surface, gasping for breath, her long eyelashes clogged with water. Like a mermaid, thought Olivier fiercely, clinging onto reason by a thread as he slid his hands beneath her arms and hauled her slippery, glistening, gorgeous body upwards in a shower of water, and then moved round so she was beneath him.

She wrapped her legs around him, pulling him onto her, and he entered her with a single hard thrust, sending a tidal wave of water crashing over the side of the bath. Gazing down into her unfocused, melting eyes was almost enough to bring him to a shuddering climax, even without the ravenous bliss of her slippery wetness around him, gripping him. He dropped his head to her breast, hearing her wild moan close to his ear as he took her deep pink nipple in his mouth.

The water slapped and sucked around them as they moved together, so deeply connected that it was impossible to tell where each of them ended and the other began. Bella's face was flushed and hazy with desire, but perfectly composed as she looked steadily, helplessly up at him. Her fingers tangled and twisted in his hair, and then suddenly let go. She lifted her arms above her head, stretching and arching, and then brought them down again to grip the iron-hard strength of his upper arms, anchoring herself as shockwaves of rapture shook her.

She clung to him in the aftermath, and Olivier buried his face in her damp neck and surrendered control. As he sank down on top of her he had the strangest sensation of having come home.

Afterwards, they lay back in the water and drank cold Muscadet from misted glasses as their pulses slowed and the darkness beyond the steamed-up window deepened. Reality had faded to a distant blur, and the future, other people, and ordinary things like work and routine were remote and incomprehensible.

Olivier's arm cradled her, holding her, his thumb gently

stroking her hand, her wrist. Feeling the thin ridge of scar tissue on the paper-fine skin, he lifted her hand in a shower of crystal droplets and looked at the pinkish scar, then pressed his lips against it.

Neither of them spoke. It was as if a fragile enchantment lay on the gentle, soft-edged world and neither of them wanted to break it.

CHAPTER TWELVE

OLIVIER stared detachedly at his BlackBerry.

For the first time ever the numbers didn't automatically make sense, and he found himself frowning, trying to process the information in front of him. In his business billions could be made or lost in the blink of an eye; he'd been out of touch with the markets for too long, and a lot had happened since he'd last checked that morning.

Not only in the financial world.

With an impatient sigh he scrolled through again, forcing his mind back into the familiar zone and laboriously checking the columns of figures. Nothing was amiss, the markets were all reasonably good. He'd taken his hand from the controls for a while, but things hadn't crashed and burned without him.

This time.

He couldn't afford to do it again. Fund management wasn't for part-timers, or people whose priorities were elsewhere. That was why he'd always been so good at it—because making money had always been his only goal.

It was what drove him. The need to escape from all this, and to prove himself. Make himself.

He set his BlackBerry down and looked around the low, lamplit kitchen. The scent of woodsmoke drifted in from the fire he had lit in the sitting room beyond, and steam misted the windows, hiding the darkness of the chilly night outside behind a diaphanous veil of silver. Upstairs he could hear the ancient floorboards creak softly as Bella moved about.

It was a world away from the sleek efficiency of the Park Lane apartment, or the opulent comforts of the villas he owned in St Tropez and Mustique, where he took whichever woman was currently top of his speed-dial list for a week of sex and sun whenever he felt like it.

Which wasn't that often. The women always resented the time he spent working, and he resented the time when he wasn't. They always seemed to expect something more than was on offer, and their flattery and suffocating affection, in such close quarters and without any distraction, grated on his nerves.

Because, he realised with a wrench, neither seemed to be related at all to him. Those women hadn't even glimpsed the real him, but had fallen in love with the monster he'd created; the hard-working, hard-hearted man who paid, paid, paid but gave nothing that mattered. Nothing of himself.

They were worshipping a cardboard cut-out. An effigy.

He scooped up the handful of mushrooms he'd picked earlier on the way back from the boathouse and unhooked a knife from beside the range. Its handle was wooden, worn smooth with age, but it fitted his hand in a way that the expensive, state-of-the-art titanium and steel ones in his own kitchen didn't. As far as he could remember, anyway. He couldn't recall the last time he had used one, or cooked anything more than just an omelette.

And he knew then that he hadn't made it at all. He'd lost himself. Lost touch with his roots and the person he was in some hollow quest for status and power. He'd denied and despised his background, and he'd subconsciously surrounded himself with people who would feel the same. For a moment he imagined bringing one of those other women here, where there was no plunge pool or home cinema… No steam room or in-house chef…

The idea was so unimaginably preposterous it was laughable. 'You're cooking?'

He looked up. Bella was standing in the doorway, her dark hair slicked back, her skin still dewy and flushed from the bath, and from their delicious lovemaking. She was wearing a grey T-shirt of Olivier's, which fell to mid-thigh, and the rest of her long, honey-coloured legs were gloriously bare.

Olivier felt his heart skip. Which was odd, he thought sardonically. Traditionally his response to a beautiful girl wearing hardly anything would have been a lot less poetic.

'You sound surprised,' he said dryly. Not entirely fairly, either, considering he'd just been thinking himself that it was pretty unusual these days.

She came to stand beside him. She didn't touch him, but he could feel his skin tingle in anticipation, almost as if it were willing her to.

She smiled. 'Impressed.' She picked up one of the big, dark-gilled mushrooms, and he watched as she stroked her fingers over its domed cap, then lifted it up to her nose and breathed in. Its damp softness and the musky, earthy scent that clung to it was unbearably sensual. Olivier had to turn away, clenching his jaw and picking up the knife to stop him sliding his hands beneath her T-shirt and having her again, right there on the floor.

'I can't believe that on top of all your other amazing talents you can cook as well.'

His voice was brusque as he began to slice the mushrooms with ruthless focus. 'When I was growing up it was a case of cook or starve. Julien wasn't very domesticated.'

'What about your mother?'

The knife stilled for a second. 'She left when I was about two.'

The steel in his voice made Bella wince. She longed to reach out to him, but his unsmiling self-possession didn't invite sympathy. She leaned against the table and looked down. 'Oh. I'm sorry, I shouldn't have asked. You don't have to talk about it.'

He swept the mushrooms into a frying pan, where almost immediately they began to soften and wilt. 'No big deal. She was doing an art history postgraduate course in Paris. She'd read about my father's work and decided to do her final year dissertation on him. She came here to see him. It was such a long time since he'd given up painting properly, and I imagine it was fairly bleak for him, so I suppose the attention flattered him—especially as she was so interested in his work. She tracked down quite a lot of the paintings he'd sold before the fire, and was interested in getting an exhibition for him, but all that came to nothing when she got pregnant.'

He paused and poured wine into the pan which hissed and sizzled, releasing a cloud of fragrant steam. Bella, silently aching for him, didn't dare speak.

'It was doomed from the start. I think she thought she could heal him and make him love her, but there was never any chance of that.'

'Why not?'

The steady, rhythmic motion of the spoon didn't falter as it turned over glossy pearls of rice in the pan. 'Because he was still in love with Genevieve. No one else would ever come close. He saw in my mother an opportunity to deaden the loneliness for a while, I suppose.' Olivier glanced up at her and gave a twisted half-smile. 'He used her. But he certainly ended up paying the price.'

'What do you mean?'

'She left, and he ended up with a child he never wanted from a woman he didn't love.'

The bland words, spoken so nonchalantly, gave Bella an insight into the bleak emotional landscape of Olivier's childhood. She shivered. She'd been so quick to jump to conclusions, so damning in her accusations that he'd neglected his father, when maybe the real story was quite the reverse.

'But your father must have loved you?' she said uncertainly. 'If he was lonely, a child must have been such a blessing. Were you never close?'

'I don't think he had much love left for anything after Genevieve Delacroix. His love for her was…total. That's why he stayed here.'

'In case she came back?'

'Partly that. Partly because he didn't want it to seem in any way like he had anything to be ashamed of.'

'In what way?'

'You believed what your uncle said, didn't you? That he'd tried to blackmail them and bring shame upon them. He knew that if he left it would look like he was guilty, that those rumours that they put around were true. So he stayed.'

'That must have taken courage,' Bella said in a small voice. 'Such a lot of courage, to stay when they had made it deliberately hard to do so.'

Olivier frowned. He'd never thought of it like that. To him, his father's passive acceptance of the situation, his tacit martyrdom, had always seemed like the ultimate act of submission. He had thought that by choosing to leave he was the courageous one.

But he'd just been running away—from the past and his problems and himself. He had been so focused on making himself as 'good' as the Delacroixes that he'd overlooked his father's far more genuine goodness.

He could see now how wrong he'd been.

'I'm so sorry, Olivier. It seems that my family have cast a long shadow over your life. I had no idea.'

'It doesn't matter any more. It's in the past.'

The words came out almost without him thinking about it. But the oddest thing was he thought he might believe them.

They ate sitting on the floor in front of the fire, in an atmosphere of quiet, bruised tenderness. Neither of them spoke much.

Bella set her plate down with a wistful sigh and leaned back against Julien's enormous old sofa. 'That was utterly delicious—thank you. I wouldn't even know where to start, especially with finding the mushrooms and everything. How do you know which ones are safe to eat?'

Olivier shrugged nonchalantly. 'I don't. I just guessed.'

Bella sat bolt-upright in horror. 'Oh, my God, Olivier—you didn't, did you? They could have been poisonous! I don't believe it—'

She stopped mid-sentence. In the glow of the fire she saw the lazy, heartbreakingly sexy smile that had spread across his face. 'You're teasing me, aren't you?' she said indignantly, leaning over to hit him playfully. 'You *do* know!'

'Of course. I grew up here, remember? You can take the boy out of rural Normandy and dress him in a suit,' he said sardonically. 'But can you ever really take rural Normandy out of the boy?'

She collapsed against him, and he moved his arm so she was lying with her head against his chest. It felt so good, so very, very good, that she was almost scared to move or breathe in case it broke the spell and he got up, or pushed her away.

'No. I don't think you can. The very first moment I saw you in that awful stuffy auction house I think that's what I sensed in you.'

'What? My peasant blood?' he said with heavy irony.

'No! Your…earthiness. Your barely concealed contempt for the bespoke suit and the silk tie. Later on I thought that you were a loner, but now I've seen where you come from I understand—that's not it. You're not a loner…you're self-sufficient. You can survive and adapt to anything, no matter what, and you don't need anyone else.'

There was a small pause. A log fell in the grate, and the wind rattled the ancient windows.

'Perhaps,' he said quietly, almost as if he wasn't aware he was speaking aloud.

Holding her against him, Olivier ran his other hand wearily

across his face, feeling the rasp of stubble against his palm, then he picked up her hand and closed his fingers around her wrist like a bracelet. In the firelight the scars were thin lines of silver on her golden skin, barely noticeable.

But he felt them.

'You're a survivor too.' His throat felt tight. 'Tell me what happened, Bella. What made you do this?'

She went very still for a moment, and then he felt the gentle rise and fall of her ribs as she sighed. 'Total bloody despair. And shame, and guilt, and humiliation…' She laughed softly. 'Shall I go on?'

'Yes. But first go back. To the beginning.'

Beneath his chin her hair felt like spun silk, and he could smell the delicate jasmine scent of her. She suddenly seemed so agonizingly, infinitely precious that he almost didn't want to hear what she was going to say because the thought of anyone hurting her crucified him.

'The beginning,' she said quietly. 'I'm not even sure where the beginning was. Not feeling that I belonged, I suppose. I've always known that I come from an important family—I remember seeing my grandfather's picture on the front of the newspaper when I was very little. But, unlike Miles, I wasn't really interested in why it was there. Miles was the clever one, the ambitious one. Compared to him I was a bitter disappointment.'

She lapsed into silence. Stroking her arm with his thumb, Olivier waited.

'Going to art school was the only thing I wanted to do,' she said after a while. 'I had to fight so hard for my parents to even consider it—they wanted me to do something *sensible*, but for the first time in my life I stood up to them. It was worth it. They made it clear that they had massive reservations, but eventually they agreed. God, I was so ecstatic.' He could hear the smile in her voice. 'I finally felt like I'd found myself. I had friends. I was living the life I wanted, doing something I was good at, and I was no longer in Miles's shadow. And then I met Dan Nightingale.'

The fragile joy that had shimmered in her voice was suddenly gone.

'He was doing a postgrad in printmaking and was one of those people that everyone knew. He was always surrounded by models and musicians, and doing glamorous, daring things. Out of nowhere he seemed to notice me—he just came up to me one afternoon as I was leaving the studio and asked me to go for a drink with him.'

'Inspired,' Olivier murmured scathingly, his fingers unconsciously tightening on her wrist as murderous loathing enveloped him.

'I was so flattered to be singled out like that. I guess because I'd stepped so far out of my family's sphere of influence it never crossed my mind that he would be aware of me as a *Lawrence*. I was ridiculously naïve, and a complete push-over. He was my f-first…proper boyfriend and I just fell for him completely. I thought he felt the same. I thought he was interested in me for *me*. And then…'

A convulsive tremor shook her whole body, and Olivier tightened his arm around her as if he could fend off the hurt. 'It was him, wasn't it?' His voice was almost a snarl. 'He was the one who took the photographs. Who made the prints.'

'How did you guess?' she said with bleak sarcasm. 'It turned out that he didn't care about me in the slightest, most insignificant bit. I was a means to an end—in this case a clever and controversial degree show exhibition—and he used me without a moment's hesitation. To him, like everyone else, I was a *name*. That's all. I was a *Lawrence*.' She gave a short gust of laughter. 'It was a valuable lesson. It made me confront the thing I'd been trying to deny all my life.'

'Which was?'

'That no matter how much I struggle to be myself and be seen as an individual I'm not. I'm someone's granddaughter, someone's daughter, someone's sister, first and foremost.'

Staring straight ahead into the fire, Olivier felt his jaw tense and his chest constrict. *No*, he wanted to say. *That's not true.* But the words lodged in his aching throat. How could he argue when he'd been guilty of seeing her like that himself?

'What I did was stupid. I know that now.' He couldn't see her face, but he felt her fingers twist into the front of his shirt. 'But I was so *hurt*—inside—and I think on some strange, confused level I wanted to bring that hurt out and make it visible, palpable. I don't remember much about it, except a mild surprise at the time that the sacred Lawrence blood looked much like anyone else's. And then Miles was there, and he...he took care of everything.'

The fire had burnt down, so that all that was left were white-hot embers, edged with coppery gold. They had been sitting there a long time. Olivier's torn back had stiffened, and when he flexed his shoulders he felt needles of agony pierce his flayed skin. He focused on the pain. His punishment.

His due.

'It seems I owe Miles an apology.' He spoke through clenched teeth. 'I was wrong about him.'

And just about everything else too.

Bella sighed. 'I know he's controlling and overbearing, but he worries about me. If it wasn't for him I wouldn't be here now.'

The flash of pain that sliced through Olivier as he bent to kiss the top of her head had nothing to do with his lacerated back.

'Then I owe him a thank-you, too,' he rasped.

Tipping his head back against the battered old sofa, he closed his eyes and picked his way through the ruins of everything he'd thought he knew or believed. Profound gratitude was not something he had ever expected to feel in relation to Miles Lawrence, but it was as if a cyclone had ripped through his head, laying waste to his entire mental landscape.

Instinctively he'd hated Dan Nightingale the moment he'd seen him with Bella in the Tate—that much was familiar. But the thing that killed him was that he was just as bad.

And he hated himself much, much more.

CHAPTER THIRTEEN

IN THE pale and glimmering light of early morning Bella woke, and instantly she knew that Olivier was gone. She struggled upright, frowning sleepily as she saw the space in the bed that still bore the imprint of his body, but the crumpled sheets— evidence of last night's quiet, intense passion—were cold.

She threw the covers back and got out of bed, feeling her heart start to hammer with nameless anguish. The house was filled with the hazy shadows of dawn so that everything seemed dissolving and insubstantial. It was as if someone had rubbed a finger over a charcoal drawing, blurring and smudging until there were no hard lines or angles.

'Olivier?'

It was barely more than a whisper, and the old walls absorbed it as she stood shivering at the top of the stairs, straining to hear in the silence some sound that would tell her he was there. None came. But then, looking up, she caught a glimpse of movement through a half-open door opposite.

On soft bare feet she approached. Standing at the window, Olivier was looking out at the blue-grey layers of mist that lay like veils over the fields. He was wearing jeans but his back was bare.

Suddenly she was reminded of the time in his apartment, when she had seen him silhouetted against the thousand brilliant, jewel-bright lights of London and had thought he looked so invincible, so wholly in command of it all. Now, just for a second, with the soft pearl-grey light of dawn falling on his shoulders, the lacerations on his back still painful and raw, she saw a nakedness and a vulnerability in him that took her breath away.

Without being conscious of deciding to do it, she found herself crossing the room to him, sliding her hands around his waist and folding herself around his body, echoing but reversing the position in which they'd finally fallen asleep last night.

'What are you doing?' she whispered.

'I have to go.'

Pressed against his back, she felt the deep rumble of his voice vibrate through her. But the closeness couldn't stop the chill from creeping into her when she heard those words, and the distant way in which he spoke them.

'Where?'

Gently, firmly, he disentangled himself from her embrace and turned so he was facing her. His face was blank, his dark eyes deeply shadowed.

'Paris. I have to see someone…about this.'

She watched him reach for what looked like a roll of stiff fabric from on top of a dusty chest of drawers. His expression didn't change as he unrolled it and spread it out in front of her.

La Dame de la Croix.

It was just as Olivier had shown her in the boathouse yesterday, and yet fundamentally different for being painted. Time stalled and logic faded, so that for the strangest moment she couldn't have said whether it was Genevieve's eyes or her own that gazed out from it so steadily, filled with quiet, triumphant repletion, with the Delacroix cross on its velvet ribbon resting crookedly on her breast.

'Oh, Olivier…it's magnificent,' she breathed. 'It's… *breathtaking.*'

'Yes,' he said simply.

'And it was lost for all these years. How wonderful that you found it and brought it back here.'

'And that I found you at the same time.'

'Fate. Or destiny,' she said softly, lifting a hand and skimming her fingertips lightly over his torn back as emotion knotted in her throat. She frowned. 'But I'm worried that we're also destined to hurt you.'

His eyes found hers and for a long moment they gazed at each other. His face wore that expression of pained intensity that carved deep lines between his brows and made her want to kiss them away. Slowly he shook his head.

'You've been hurt too, but it's over now. All of that is in the past.'

There was a quiet ferocity in his voice, so the words sounded more like a vow than a statement. Fear wrapped icy fingers around Bella's heart and squeezed, stalling her breath. She just wanted to be held against him, safe in his arms, but Olivier had already moved away and was putting on his shirt.

Dressed, he seemed suddenly distant from her—as if, wherever he was going, he had somehow already left.

Driving away from the mill, Bella's kiss still warm on his lips in the chilly dawn, Olivier felt impatience rise up inside him. He tensed his grip on the steering wheel and pressed his foot even harder on the accelerator.

He'd barely even left and already he couldn't wait to get back. *Home.* And that was something he'd never believed he'd catch himself thinking.

Last night, as Bella had rested her head on his chest in the fire-light, he'd glimpsed a peace that had eluded him for a lifetime. He'd felt whole—as if the sharp, disjointed fragments that formed him had finally merged. For a brief time she'd made him feel good about himself, about who he was—and the mill and the past and his distant, difficult, damaged father were all part of that. She had accepted it all so easily, and it suddenly seemed pitiful that he had never been able to accept it himself.

He could now. Thanks to her, he wasn't ashamed any more—not of his past. But the horrific irony was that what he had done to her at the beginning now made a far darker stain on his conscience.

He had set out to hurt her, to do exactly the same thing as that bastard who had exploited her before. And although he was prepared to spend however long it took making up to her for it, he wouldn't get the chance if he didn't stop Veronique Lemercier's damned article.

In a couple of days the big Delacroix scandal of fifty years ago—the affair, the painting, the fire, the blackmail—would be gripping intelligent middle-class professionals all over France and England as they ate their cornflakes. For as long as he could remember, more than anything else, he'd wanted the world to know what Philippe Delacroix and Edward Lawrence had done, but all of a sudden there was something he wanted more.

To protect Bella.

At Rouen Hospital, morning visiting hadn't started, but when Olivier tersely explained that he had to talk to his father on an urgent matter the ward sister agreed to let him in. Julien was awake, and Olivier felt a sharp stab of guilt as he noticed the way the old man's eyes lit up when he saw him.

He frowned, struggling to know where to begin bridging the wide chasm that lay between them, forged by a lifetime of mis-understanding. Julien's scarred hands lay folded awkwardly on the bed, livid and shocking against the smooth white sheet.

Hesitantly Olivier placed his own over them. It was as good a place as any to start.

The sun was warm on her back when Bella turned the MG into the rutted driveway of the mill at lunchtime. It was another of those ravishing autumn days when everything seemed to be brushed with gold dust, and she found she was smiling as she turned the key in the heavy door, her arms laden with packages. She felt, bizarrely, as if she was coming home.

The now-familiar scent of woodsmoke and apples enveloped her as she crossed the warm flagstones of the hallway and went into the kitchen, depositing her armful of purchases on the table. It seemed incredible to think that she had come here so unexpectedly—and reluctantly—but that the moment when she'd first set foot in this crooked, creaking old building it had been almost as if she'd stepped into an enchantment.

This was where she'd discovered herself…and Olivier, and she knew without being able to say how or why that it couldn't have happened anywhere else.

Absentmindedly she sorted through the assortment of packages on the table. She'd had a surprisingly successful morning. Not wanting to hang around alone after Olivier had left for Paris, she had dressed and driven to a small town about ten kilometres away, where one of the markets on Celia's list was held. Her early start had been richly rewarded, and the boot of the MG was now full of brown paper parcels containing bone-white antique linen sheets, feather bolster cushions covered in vintage ticking, a couple of curled wire planters, and four exceptionally gorgeous silvered glass candlesticks for Miles and Ashley, twisted like barley sugar and glistening like moonlit frost. The perfect wedding gift. Bella knew that Ashley would love them.

But that wasn't what was causing the smile to keep returning to her face. Her hands were trembling slightly as she picked up one flat, tissue-wrapped parcel and peeled back the rustling layers with impatient fingers. The smile broadened as she smoothed back the last layer of tissue and picked up the richly-embroidered silk, shaking it out and watching its luscious colours spring to life in the sunlit kitchen.

It was Olympia's shawl.

And suddenly she was back in the Tate, with Olivier standing beside her, his lips brushing her palm, her neck. Her own words came back to her, and the sound of her own voice—husky with desire. *I…love…the shawl…I can imagine how the silk must feel against her skin…*

Tonight maybe she would find out for real.

She stood still, clutching the chilly silk to her as a wave of lust and longing crashed through her, nearly knocking her sideways. Last night's lovemaking in the creaking old brass bed had been both tender and intense, and she shivered as she recalled the new sensations he had awoken in her hungry, questing body. Lit only by the moon, his face had been as impassive and remote as ever, but his body had told a different story, and as she had taken him in her mouth and let her tongue explore and caress she had felt his control slip away. He had gripped her and cried out her name as if he were in pain.

But, Bella thought firmly, dragging herself back to the present and folding up the shawl, there had been enough of that. Enough pain, enough suffering. Now it was time for healing and for pleasure…Starting tonight, when he got back from Paris.

She had bought ingredients for dinner from a friendly *boucherie,* and intended to spend the afternoon cooking for him. The problem of mastering the range terrified her, but other than that the prospect of such quiet, intimate domesticity was profoundly, almost guiltily delicious. Firstly she would lay a fire for later, and make a start.

The sitting room was grey and full of shadows. Bella swept out the ash and brought in more logs to replenish the basket beside the huge stone fireplace, then looked around for newspaper to lay a new one. Julien must keep them somewhere especially for the purpose, but she hadn't come across them so far…

On the lowest shelf of the huge wooden bookcase that ran

almost the length of one wall she saw a large box and, peering inside, was pleased to see a stack of newspapers. She pulled out the top one, and was about to start scrunching it up for kindling when something made her stop.

The paper was brittle and yellowed with age, and she noticed that the date at the top of the page was November 1954.

A sense of chilly foreboding stole through her as her eyes scanned the front page.

The name leapt out at her instantly, as if it had been printed in foot-high crimson letters.

DELACROIX.

Bella sat back on her heels and ran her hands through her hair. Letting them drop back into her lap, she found they were shaking. For a moment she sat perfectly still in the centre of the soft and faded rug where she and Olivier had lain last night, then she took all of the newspapers from the box.

She let out a small whimper of distress as she found another article in the next one. And the next.

Wrapping her arms around herself, she began to read.

The sun had been swallowed up by massing ranks of black clouds by the time Bella got unsteadily to her feet an hour later. She staggered a little, holding on to the bookcase for support as the blood seeped painfully back into her feet and her shocked brain struggled to assimilate all she'd just learned.

And then, bending down, she swept the scattered papers into her arms and grabbed the keys to the MG. She was white-lipped with anger.

Philippe Delacroix might have used bribery and blackmail to ensure he didn't have to answer for what he'd done to Julien in a court of law, but she was going to make him confront it now.

CHAPTER FOURTEEN

LEANING across a desk cluttered with auction catalogues and paperwork to shake the hand of the Louvre's Commissioner for Twentieth-Century Art, Olivier felt as though a great weight had been lifted from him. *La Dame de la Croix* was clipped to an easel on the other side of the room, from where Genevieve Delacroix's eyes regarded him steadily. At the door, he turned to look at it one last time.

Julien had responded to Olivier's proposition with the same calm acceptance that had enabled him to endure the other losses in his life. When Olivier had handed the painting to him he had held the roll of canvas tightly in his scarred hands, but he had not looked at it. *'There is no need,'* he had said hoarsely. *'Every detail is as vivid in my mind's eye now as it was when I painted it.'* And, recalling the image of Bella, naked and ravishing against the red velvet, Olivier had understood completely.

'Once again, *merci*, Monsieur Moreau,' the commissioner said solemnly now. 'It is a magnificent painting, and will make an extremely valuable part of our collection... in the fullness of time,' he added carefully. The terms of the donation were that *La Dame de la Croix* would not be hung until Philippe Delacroix, Genevieve Lawrence and Julien Moreau had all been dead for five years. 'Let us hope that that time does not come too soon,' he added with dutiful courtesy.

Olivier nodded briefly, his eyes still fixed on those of the woman in the painting. For a second he imagined that he saw approval there.

He walked back through the huge echoing hallways and corridors of the gallery, deliberately keeping his footsteps slow and measured, although a part of him wanted to break into a run. He had plenty of time before his lunch meeting with Veronique about pulling the article. Too much time. He felt impatient to be finished and on the way home.

Going back to Le Moulin and to Bella.

Walking along Paris's most exclusive shopping streets, he gazed unseeingly into brightly lit window displays of glittering jewellery and starkly minimalist displays of designer clothing. All of it seemed ridiculously irrelevant—a flimsy two-dimensional world of image and appearance. The world he'd used to inhabit.

But then, right in front of him, he noticed a smaller shop, squeezed between two aggressively stylish designer giants, with a narrow art nouveau frontage painted in absinthe-green. In the window were old-fashioned tailors' mannequins displaying an array of delicate lingerie in shades of turquoise and tangerine and rose.

Olivier stopped on the pavement, feeling a slow half-smile spread across his face as heat rose through his body and a kaleidoscope of luscious images rampaged through his mind.

OK, so not all the shops here were irrelevant, he thought ruefully, opening the door. This kind of shopping he could easily see the point of.

Waves…white sandy beach…palm trees…

Pacing back from the far wall to the window, Bella could feel her self-control slipping. She knew she mustn't give in to the hysteria that was lapping at her brain far more insistently than the waves on any damned white sandy beach.

She had to stay calm. Had to stay positive. Had to stay rational.

Not that there was anything remotely positive or rational about being locked in a room in a deserted château with a dangerously insane distant relative.

When she'd met him yesterday she had sensed something slightly obsessive, slightly deranged, in Philippe Delacroix's manner when he had spoken of the painting and of Julien Moreau. Not for a second, however, had she imagined the depths of that obsession or the corrosive violence of his derangement.

Obviously. If she had she would never have arrived on his doorstep with her armful of newspapers and her foolish, naïve moralising.

Her throat constricted painfully around the dry sob that rose up inside her, and for the millionth time she glanced out of the window, hoping desperately to see a black Aston Martin roaring towards the house. Where was Olivier now? Philippe had wanted her to ring him, to summon him to Le Manoir with the painting, and he hadn't believed her when she'd said she didn't know Olivier's mobile number. As she'd tried to explain to him that she and Olivier Moreau had only known each other for the shortest time, the gossamer ties that connected them had begun to feel increasingly fragile.

The fact that she didn't even know what he was doing in Paris or when he was coming back just emphasised how tenuous their relationship was. Pulling the sleeves of her jumper down over her cold, cold hands, Bella slid down the wall. As shadows gathered in the cobwebbed corners of the room she put her head on her knees and comforted herself by recalling every delicious, bone-melting moment of last night with Olivier.

It beat waves on a stupid beach any day.

Olivier had just been waiting for the girl in the shop to finish wrapping the last of his purchases in layers of pink tissue paper when his PA had called. The message she gave him had filled him with unspeakable dread.

It had seemed to take for ever to get out of Paris. Slumped helplessly behind the wheel of the Aston Martin in the midst of the Friday traffic, there was nothing to distract him from going over and over the possible implications of Philippe Delacroix's call. Alicia had said he had sounded angry and agitated, and that he wanted Olivier to go straight away to Le Manoir, where Bella was 'waiting for him'.

And he wanted him to bring the painting.

An early autumn dusk had fallen as the Aston Martin devoured the last few miles, its headlamps illuminating the gloomy, over-grown hedgerows. By the time he finally swung the car, with a screech of tyres, between the tall stone gateposts of Le Manoir, Olivier felt spacy with adrenalin. His self-control, stretched almost to breaking point on the long drive, was now hanging by a thread.

He leapt out of the car and slammed the door with barely controlled violence. He just hoped that Delacroix wasn't stupid enough to annoy him. *Or to have hurt Bella.*

That was the thought that he'd so ruthlessly squashed all the way from Paris, but now he was here it seemed to balloon hugely, blocking out everything else in his head. There was no way of rationalizing any scenario involving Bella, the painting and Philippe Delacroix. It was a combination that could only mean disaster.

Olivier's few dealings with Delacroix over Le Moulin had shown him that Genevieve's older brother had never forgotten what had happened, but instead had held onto it until it became almost an obsession. He was deluded. Deranged. And, Olivier thought with a sickening thud of anguish, very possibly dangerous.

Running up the stone steps, he applied his shoulder violently to the heavy double front doors, feeling them yield a little under the pressure. He pushed again, and the lock gave way.

The huge hallway was murky in the half-light. Striding across its chilly marble floor, Olivier shouted Bella's name. For a second he paused, listening to his voice echoing through the gloomy rooms that spread out on either side of him. And then, from somewhere up above, he thought he heard an answering call.

Relief shot through him, searing and pure. He was halfway up the wide staircase when a voice came from behind him.

'Really, Monsieur Moreau. Your manners are every bit as deplorable as your vulgar father's. Don't you know that in polite society we knock before entering?'

Olivier stopped and turned slowly round. Philippe Delacroix stood in the shadows at the foot of the stairs, looking up at him. He was dressed for the outdoors—as if he was on some shooting party from the days before the Great War, with plus fours and gaiters and a tweed jacket.

For a split second Olivier felt a flash of pity for the relic he had become. And then loathing obliterated everything.

'Where's Bella?' he said icily.

'She's waiting for you. You can see her once you've handed over what I asked for.' Delacroix spoke completely matter-of-factly, as if they were discussing a dog. 'I trust you brought the painting, as instructed. If not, I am afraid Bella will have to wait longer, and she won't like that at all. She is like my sister—very impatient.' His lips drew back and he gave a sudden burst of wheezing laughter. 'And with a similar penchant for the lower orders.'

Hitting him, going down the stairs and knocking Philippe Delacroix across his own stately hallway, would be the most tempting thing in the world, but at that moment Olivier heard a noise from along the corridor at the top of the stairs: the rattling of a door handle, accompanied by a muffled voice.

Bella's voice.

In an instant he was at the top of the stairs, striding quickly along the dim corridor. Following the sound of her voice, he pushed open doors, calling to her. At last he came to a locked door.

'Olivier! I'm here!'

'Stand back from the door,' he snarled, his voice harsh with anxiety.

It didn't give way as easily as the front door had done—locked with an old-fashioned key, it proved much more durable than the more modern latch downstairs—but the urgent need to get to Bella doubled Olivier's already considerable strength. On the fourth attempt there was a splintering of wood and the door burst open.

And she was there. Bella was there. She was standing in the centre of the empty room, her hands pressed to her mouth, her blue eyes wide with fear and joy and relief. For a moment neither of them moved. Their eyes met, and Olivier had to brace himself as a tidal wave of totally unfamiliar emotion battered him. He held back, suddenly afraid that if he went to her then he wouldn't be able to stop himself from crushing her to him and kissing the living daylights out of her.

'You came,' she croaked. 'I'm so sorry, I—'

She broke off as a hidden door in the panelling behind her opened and, like a pantomime villain, Philippe Delacroix appeared.

'*Alors*—I said to *wait*.'

It would have been farcical but for the fact there was something very sinister about the soft, reasonable tone of Philippe's voice as, addressing Olivier, he took hold of Bella's arm. It took Olivier a moment to realise that in one hand he carried a rifle.

'Why is it that no one seems capable of following the simplest commands these days?' Delacroix went on in a tone of weary regret. 'No wonder society is in such a terrible mess. It was all so much easier when people listened to their betters and did as they were told.'

'What are you doing, Delacroix?'

'I told you, Moreau. I said *quite clearly* that before you could see Bella I wanted the painting.' Philippe shook his head sadly, and in the grey twilight Olivier could see the slightly manic glitter in his small eyes. 'You may think you can get away with disregarding my orders, but you are wrong.'

'I haven't got the painting,' Olivier said tersely.

Bella's eyes blazed into his in the dingy room. 'He knows you have, Olivier. I told him. I'm so sorry—I didn't know…I didn't think…'

'See?' Delacroix said triumphantly, flinging his arms out, so that the gun made a wide arc, glinting dully in the gloom. 'There's no point in *lying*, Moreau. You have what I want and…' with one hand he waved the gun at Bella '…I have what you want. It's a very simple transaction. You give me that painting and I give you your girl.'

Olivier's mind raced. Narrowing his eyes, he measured the distance between them. He was too far away to snatch the gun, and any sudden movement would be unwise; Philippe Delacroix was a renowned shot. But he had to find some way of distracting him long enough to get Bella to safety.

Nonchalantly he shrugged. 'OK. I admit I have it. But I'm not letting it go.'

He heard Bella's soft gasp of dismay. Not looking at her, not reaching out to her then, took strength of Herculean proportions.

Bella felt dread prickle through every nerve and cell, like poison, until she thought she might black out. She kept her eyes fixed on Olivier's, trying to anchor herself in him as the shadows darkened at the edges of her vision, but the expression of cold hauteur on his face chilled her like death.

She hardly noticed the barrel of the gun pressing into her ribs.

'Think very carefully about that, Moreau,' rasped Philippe in a voice that made Bella's flesh crawl. Olivier half turned away.

'No need, I'm afraid,' he said coldly. 'The deal is off, Delacroix.

I spent years looking for that painting, and I'm not about to give it up. For anyone.'

Bella clasped her hands together to stop them shaking, tucking them beneath her chin as her eyes were stretched wide by shock and horror. Dimly she was aware of Philippe's discomfiture, the sharp jab of the rifle beneath her diaphragm, but it paled into insignificance in the face of Olivier's betrayal.

'So you used her, just like your father used my sister,' Philippe hissed venomously.

Time stood still. A thick, muffling silence fell over the lightless room. Bella felt as if she was under water. Everything seemed to slow and stall as she waited for Olivier to speak. To deny it.

'Yes. I used her.'

He was frowning slightly, and in the gathering dusk he looked entirely remote. In that instant it was impossible to imagine kissing that brutal, beautiful mouth or gripping those massive, powerful shoulders as she shivered and melted in ecstasy. His cruel words, spoken so casually, fell on her like careless hammer blows and it was as if she had dreamed it all.

'I used her to get back at you,' he went on offhandedly, taking a step towards them. 'I simply wanted to take what had been forbidden to my father. It was revenge—pure and simple.'

Bella heard her own low moan of pain, but was suddenly aware that the gun was no longer pressing into her. And then it all happened very quickly—small, individual actions all crowding in on each other so that it was impossible to make sense of any of them. She saw a glint of metal, felt the sudden, erratic movement of Philippe beside her, heard his low grunt of rage as he swung the gun towards Olivier.

And she felt as if her heart was being wrenched from inside her as she watched, in slow motion, Olivier lurch towards him, his arm coming out to knock the gun from Philippe's wild, shaking grasp. His face showed no emotion.

There was a noise. Louder than anything Bella had ever heard before. Too loud to be anything other than very, very real.

And then Olivier was falling, and a vivid scarlet stain was spreading on the front of his shirt.

Above his heart.

CHAPTER FIFTEEN

EVERYTHING felt unreal. Like a dream. Or a film.

Before the echo of the single gunshot had died away Bella was dropping to her knees beside Olivier, her fingers fluttering over his neck, searching for a pulse as the crimson stain grew on the white of his shirt like some terrible flower unfurling its petals.

His skin was warm, and bending closer she caught the delicious familiar scent of him above the reek of cordite. She closed her eyes and gave a gasp of relief as she felt the rapid flicker of his pulse.

Opening them again, she glanced up. Philippe was standing motionless, the arm holding the gun held stiffly out at an odd, unnatural angle, almost as if he were trying to pretend it wasn't part of him. His face, she dimly registered, was grey and crumpled with shock, but there was no space in her head for him now.

It was too full of Olivier.

Olivier, Olivier, Olivier, whose exceptional face was now an unearthly chalk-white in the dying light. Olivier, whose blood was warm on her hands. Olivier, who didn't love her.

Who had used her.

And in the whole nightmarish scene this was the only thing that seemed real, the only fact her frozen brain could fix on with any certainty.

She bent over him, her numb fingers clumsily searching for his mobile phone in the inside pocket of his jacket. Finding it, she took it out and looked at it in blank panic, not knowing how to make it work.

'Here…'

Olivier's eyes were open. His voice was just a cracked whisper, but it had lost none of its force. Even lying bleeding on the floor he was still powerful, still somehow in command. With mammoth effort his hand came up and she put the phone into it, and then, his jaw clenching with pain, he raised his head. Mutely Bella cradled him on her knees as he pressed buttons, then held the phone out for her to take.

For the second time in as many days Bella found herself requesting an ambulance. She only hoped this one would arrive more quickly, and anguish swelled inside her as she watched Olivier's eyes flicker closed again. She didn't know how long he could hold on.

Philippe had vanished, she wasn't sure when, and now the only noise in the huge room was the unnatural sucking rasp of Olivier's breathing. She had to do something, but she felt completely powerless. As if she'd been drugged, or was being slowly pulled down by quicksand.

He didn't love her. He'd used her. It was what she'd been afraid of all along, and what she'd tried to block out, but it made perfect sense. He must have known who she was from the start. And hated her for it.

'Bella…'

He was looking up at her, his eyes burning into hers, his face filled with pain and ferocious determination. 'What—I—s-s-said…' He stopped, closing his eyes and swallowing convulsively. Every word was edged with agony, as if he had razor wire wrapped around his throat.

Instinctively she held her hand to his cheek, feeling the tense muscles beneath his stubble-roughened jaw. 'Shhh…' she murmured automatically, shaking her head. 'Don't speak.'

Panic was beginning to break through the anaesthetizing shock. She could feel his chest heaving with the effort of forcing the air in and out of his lungs. Not knowing what else to do, she hurriedly undid the buttons of his shirt, peeling it back from the torn and bloodied flesh beneath.

For the briefest fraction of a second she was struck by how beautiful he was. His skin was bleached of all colour—even his lovely mouth was pale—so that he looked like a marble effigy of some knight crusader. The splash of scarlet on the white of his skin was strangely lovely.

Almost instantly the reality of the situation assailed her. She bent over him in the gathering dusk and focused all her energy on biting back the whimper of distress that threatened to escape her. She kept her face expressionless as she looked at the wound, but behind her impassive mask she raged with panic and terror. *God, oh, please, God—what should I do…?*

'Stop the—blood.'

It was as if she'd spoken out loud. Olivier's voice was like sandpaper, and his eyes stayed closed. But he was still with her. He was still there. And he was still strong.

'Tell me what to do,' she said through frozen lips. 'Tell me, Olivier.'

'Press—hard.'

She felt his icy-cold fingers close around her hand and, lifting it, he placed it over his heart.

Pure astringent agony sliced into her, scalpel-sharp, making her gasp.

It didn't matter if he loved her or not. The fact was she loved him, and she was as helpless to stop that as she was to stop the blood that was seeping through her fingers. And it hurt just as much.

Gradually his face relaxed, and the lines of pain between his brows slowly faded. As minutes passed and the corners of the room were lost in the gathering twilight, Bella's hand grew numb with pressing, and her world shrank to nothing but the rapid beat of his heart and the hoarse suck of his breath.

When she saw the neon blue light of the approaching ambulance flickering over the bare walls there was a tiny, shameful corner of her mind that was disappointed. Because now she'd have to let him go.

Olivier drifted in and out of a place where everything was dark and there was nothing but physical sensation. He felt the hard floor against his back, the cold stealing into his bones, Bella's hand, warm and soft as angel's wings, against his cheek.

And the pain, of course. He felt that. The pain suffused everything, like smoke. It curled around him until he could no longer separate anything out from it. Breathing. Moving. Speaking.

He needed to speak. He had to make sure that Bella knew what he'd said to Delacroix wasn't true. But it was hard to breathe, very hard, and he knew that he needed to keep as still as possible and use his oxygen wisely if he was to stand a chance of surviving until help arrived.

He had to survive, because there was so much he still wanted to do. And say.

I love you.

Summoning all his strength, he opened his eyes a little. Blue lights sliced crazily through the dark fog around him and there was noise. Voices. Footsteps vibrating on the floorboards. Bella's face swam above him. It was pale and perfectly beautiful, and it glistened with tears.

He frowned.

'Don't—cry…' His chest felt as if it was on fire, and the words seemed to scour the raw flesh like acid, but he had to say them. He gathered his failing strength. 'I—'

But she was pulling away from him. 'It's time,' she whispered. 'They're here, Olivier.'

He felt a shot of heat in his arm, and the darkness came back.

Time did strange things in situations of great awfulness, Bella decided as she watched another grey dawn break. The night she had spent in the waiting room of the Paris hospital had felt like a thousand years, with the hands on the oversized clock on the wall opposite moving so slowly she'd wanted to scream. And yet yesterday morning, waking in the sagging old bed that still bore the scent of their bodies and tiptoeing through the luminescent shadows to find Olivier, seemed to have happened only moments ago.

The words she'd said to him then had echoed round her head through the long silent hours. *It seems we're destined to hurt you.* Now, sitting on a hard plastic chair in the empty waiting room, they seemed like a terrible premonition.

The small hospital in Rouen had not been able to deal with Olivier's injuries. The bullet had shattered his ribs and punctured a lung and, although they could stabilise him in the ambulance, he needed surgery immediately. Bella had followed behind the ambulance in a police car, and throughout the dark journey the only emotion to penetrate the thick blanket of numbness in her head had been guilt.

The *gendarmes* were being so kind—what would they say if they found out that she was being ushered to Olivier's bedside under false pretences? He wouldn't want her to be there because he didn't love her. It was just her own selfishness, her desperate, hopeless longing to be with him for as long as possible that compelled her to follow.

A nurse with a plump, concerned face appeared in front of her now, smiling kindly. Bella kept her eyes fixed to the blank face of the clock over her shoulder, afraid that even the smallest gesture of warmth would cause the dam on her emotions to burst and the tidal wave of grief it unleashed to wash her away.

Monsieur Moreau had come round from the surgery a little while ago, the nurse explained in a slow and disjointed mixture of French and English. His injuries, though severe, were no longer life threatening, and it was a miracle that his heart had escaped completely unscathed.

Bella nodded earnestly. She had known that already, of course. It was only *her* heart that was shattered.

'He has been asking for you, *cherie*,' the nurse said gently.

Bella let her eyes flicker briefly from the hard white disc of the clock face. The nurse was looking at her with infinite compassion. 'Really?' she whispered.

The nurse's smile broadened to a beam. 'He would not lie still. When he come round from the anaesthetic, straight away he try to take out his drip and get up to see you.' She shook her head fondly. 'He keep saying he need to speak with you. He is not an easy patient, but he has the strength of ten men. He's a survivor, *c'est vrai.*'

As she hurried along the corridor to Olivier's room Bella was horribly aware of her unwashed face and creased, day-old clothes, and also of the fragile spark of hope that the nurse's words had ignited. Tethered to machines and tubes, Olivier lay sleeping again, and she felt scoured out and weak with love as she looked down into his peaceful face.

Tentatively she reached out her hand and stroked her fingertips along the smooth brown underside of his forearm, beneath the brutal needles that dripped fluid into his veins.

He stirred instantly, as if he had been waiting for her to call him back from whatever unreachable place he was in. Gripped by anguish, Bella watched helplessly as the shadows and pain flooded back into his face and his fingers flexed and clenched.

'*Veronique…*'

Ice dripped down Bella's spine. Her hand stayed on his arm, her fingers still stroking and caressing, but the rest of her was frozen with shock.

'I need…Veronique…'

Nausea rose up inside her. Of course the nurse had no way of knowing that Veronique wasn't *her* name; that she wasn't the one Olivier wanted to see. Horrorstruck, Bella snatched her hand away as he struggled to sit up, his fingers groping desperately at the narrow tubes, pulling at the tapes that fastened the needle into the crook of his arm. Dumbly she stepped backwards, her hands flying to cover her mouth as the machine beside him began to emit a high-pitched wail. In the bed Olivier thrashed, his face contorted with anguish and pain, the same word coming from his pale lips over and over again.

'Veronique.'

From out in the corridor there was the sound of running feet, and Bella shrank back as two nurses burst into the room and bent over Olivier, easing him back against the pillows, soothing, checking the lines and tubes and pressing buttons on the machine. Hovering in the doorway, Bella felt like an impostor.

She should go. Leave. Now. But…

'Bella? Oh, my God, darling, there you are…'

For a moment she thought exhaustion and grief had finally undone her and she was hallucinating, but she found herself being swept into a perfumed, silken embrace.

Ashley.

'Oh, sweetheart, thank goodness I found you. Miles is frantic. I came as soon as we heard about Philippe. You've been through so much, you poor, poor baby.'

As Ashley led her gently out of the room, away from Olivier, the dam inside Bella burst. She wasn't sure how long they stood there in the corridor as she wept and Ashley rocked and soothed and stroked her hair, but when she finally pulled away her eyes were swollen almost shut and Ashley's grey silk jacket was soaked with tears.

'Oh, Ash,' she croaked, 'it's all such a mess. I'm so glad you're here.'

'So am I. Come on, you need a break. I'm taking you back to my hotel for a hot bath and a good sleep. Don't even bother to argue.'

Bella bit her lip against another surge of tears and shook her head wanly.

'I wasn't going to. I'm done here. Let's go.'

'What time is it?'

Ashley smiled down at her. 'Nearly eight o'clock.'

Bella rubbed a hand across her gritty eyes and frowned. 'I've slept all day.'

'And all night, darling, thank goodness. You needed the rest.' Ashley crossed the thickly carpeted floor of the hotel suite and pulled back the curtains, letting thin sunlight flood the room. 'It's nearly eight o'clock on Sunday morning.'

Struggling upright, Bella blinked and pushed the hair back from her face as the real world reassembled itself in her consciousness. She had slept a blank, dreamless sleep, no doubt brought about by the large gin and tonic and the sleeping pill that Ashley had given her, but now the memory of yesterday began to come back to her with the same screaming pain as blood returning to a cramped limb.

'Olivier?' she croaked desperately. 'How is he?'

Perching on the edge of the bed, Ashley placed a steadying hand on Bella's shoulder. 'It's OK. Miles rang about half an hour ago, when he'd spoken to the hospital, and the news is Olivier's doing fine. It's you we're worried about.'

Bella collapsed back against the pillows and turned her face away.

'I'm all right.'

'I'm not so sure about that,' Ashley said gently. 'Bella—what happened…what you've been through…it must have been so terrible, and I know it's difficult, but it would be so much better if you could talk about it.'

'There's nothing to say except that I did it again.' Bella turned to look up at Ashley as tears slid down her face and into her hair. 'I fell for someone who was just using me. Only this time it's a thousand times worse because now I know he was in love with someone else all along. Veronique.'

Ashley frowned and shook her head in confusion. 'Darling, I don't understand. I was talking about what happened with Philippe, and the shooting…' She paused, then smoothed Bella's hair back from her damp forehead and stood up, her eyes full of concern. 'I'm going to make you a coffee, and then I think you'd better tell me everything. From the beginning.'

And so, clutching the gold-rimmed cup between her frozen hands, Bella began with that first evening in London, when Olivier had deliberately, single-mindedly, unravelled her from her cotton-wool numbness and brought her back to life, and went right up to night at the mill, where he'd held her in the firelight and listened to her as she'd bared her soul. Ashley listened without interrupting.

'It was so sudden and intense,' Bella whispered tonelessly, as Ashley gently took the now-cold coffee cup from her grasp and put it on the bedside table. 'But so right…so *perfect* that I thought it must be meant to be.' She looked up with a smile of infinite sadness. 'How ridiculous that sounds now, when I know he was putting it on the whole time. He set out deliberately to seduce me. As revenge for what my family had done to his father.'

Ashley shook her head decisively. 'I don't think so. If that was the case you would have sensed it. You would have known.'

Bella's eyes were black holes of despair. 'Why? I didn't last time, with Dan Nightingale. And Olivier *said* it, Ashley—I heard him, remember, at Le Manoir?'

For the first time a note of impatience crept into Ashley's tone. 'Give the guy a break, Bella! He was dealing with a gun-toting psycho at the time. I think that can make you say things you don't mean.'

Beneath the covers Bella drew her knees more tightly up to her body, bringing her head down onto them and squeezing her eyes closed. 'I *know*. I've thought about that,' she moaned. 'I thought that maybe it could have been part of some plan to divert Philippe's attention or something, but if it was, it was the most insane thing to do. Why would he deliberately provoke a man with a gun?'

Ashley's voice was very tender. 'Because he loves you, of course.'

For a moment Bella didn't move, or lift her head. Her hair fell forward, completely obscuring her face, and in the dark cave it created she explored what Ashley had just said. Hesitantly she looked up, trying to keep the tremulous hope from her voice.

'But Veronique… He was asking for Veronique.'

'You're jumping to conclusions, honey. She could be his sister for all you know.'

'He doesn't have a sister.'

There was a knock at the door and Ashley got up. 'OK, his secretary, then. But from what you've just told me he's worth a little faith. You at least owe him that.' She smiled, going towards the door. 'Now, here's breakfast.'

While she was gone Bella tried to make her brain accommodate this new, tempting perspective. There was a wonderful logic to Ashley's theory, but could she really allow herself to hope that—

'Bella, love? Some gentlemen to see you.'

Surprised, she looked up as Ashley ushered the two *gendarmes* who had taken Bella to the hospital the other night into the room. Seeing them in daylight, in the orderly opulence of the hotel, was seriously bizarre—like characters from a film, they belonged to a world of chaos and mess.

They had come to give Bella the news that Philippe Delacroix's body had been discovered in a disused farm building on the St Laurien estate. He had shot himself, they explained gently, and this time the bullet had been fatal.

Bella felt nothing but relief.

They had also come to give her back the keys to the MG, which had been returned to the mill, and to inform her that Olivier's Aston Martin had been collected by the hire company. Then, blushing furiously, the shorter of the two men stepped forward and held out a stiff peppermint-green carrier bag, of the kind used by extremely exclusive boutiques. Pink tissue paper frothed from the top.

'The car hire firm found this in Monsieur Moreau's car, *mademoiselle*. They asked that it be passed on to him.'

The moment they'd gone, Ashley rushed forward. 'Well, what are you waiting for? See what's in it!'

As if she'd been hypnotised Bella looked into the bag. Her face bore an expression of trepidation that suggested she was expecting to find a live snake coiled in the crisp layers of tissue. Slowly she put her hand in and drew out a delicate pink-wrapped package, as light as air.

Inside lay a pair of silk knickers in a delicious, stinging char-treuse-green. They were edged with satin ribbon the colour of kingfisher wings, and against the bright pink tissue they looked so incredibly beautiful that for a moment all either of them could do was stare.

'Oh, wow, Bella…' Ashley's voice was a wistful moan that said very clearly that Miles had never bought anything as wildly lovely as this for her. She looked at Bella in open admiration. 'This man has seriously good taste.'

One by one the packages were pulled out, and the tissue stripped back to reveal bras and knickers in Parma violet and strawberry-pink and aquamarine. Nothing matched, every silken whisper was different, and by the time they'd finished, the bed was like a molten rainbow.

'So,' said Ashley in quiet triumph, 'what does this tell you?'

Before Bella could make her dazzled brain conjure up the words to answer, they were interrupted by another knock on the door as Room Service arrived with breakfast. On the trolley with the warm croissants and fragrant coffee lay a selection of the Sunday newspapers, which Ashley tossed onto the bed, sending pieces of pink tissue fluttering in all directions, like flamingos taking flight.

'Coffee or tea?' she asked happily, and when Bella didn't answer she laughed and went on, 'Or, if you're too stunned with love to choose, would you like me to decide for you?' She poured coffee into two cups and turned round.

The smile died on her lips.

Afterwards, she described to Miles the look on Bella's face as that of someone who had just been diagnosed with a terminal illness. All the life, all the hope had been brutally extinguished, leaving her gaunt and ashen.

Instantly Ashley was beside her, following her agonised, beseeching gaze to the newspaper that lay face-up on the bed. For a moment they both just stared, transfixed with shock, at the picture that covered most of the front page. *La Dame de la Croix,* her luminous glory only slightly dimmed in newsprint, stared serenely up at them, almost mocking them with her composure.

'How did they…? Who could have…?'

Ashley's incredulous question died on her lips as she noticed what Bella had seen already: the name beneath the headline.

Veronique Lemercier.

With a succinct curse Ashley made a grab for the paper, but Bella was too quick for her. Snatching it up, she clutched it to her with the sadistic ferocity of an alcoholic seizing the last bottle of gin in the shop.

'Bella, don't read it—please. Let me…'

'No!' Bella spat. She was white and shaking, but her eyes burned with a forceful intensity. Ashley knew there was no point in arguing. She watched helplessly as Bella spread out the paper with trembling hands and began to read. With a terrible sense of foreboding she moved closer and scanned the print from above Bella's bent head.

Veronique Lemercier was 'a long-standing intimate acquaintance' of Olivier Moreau, the introduction to the article stated. Ashley heard Bella's ragged gasp of pain as she read this, and her heart bled for her. She wanted to pick up the paper and tear it into a thousand pieces, but she knew that wouldn't help. It was too late to take refuge in ignorance now. Taking a deep breath, she forced herself to read on.

It was all exactly as Bella had feared. Veronique's article described in moving detail how she had helped Olivier Moreau in his single-minded quest to find the only painting to survive the fire that had destroyed his father's career and prevented him from achieving the greatness and recognition he so deserved.

Halfway down the page, Ashley stopped reading and swore quietly. She realised, distantly, that her hands were clenched into fists and the nails were digging into her palms. Beside her, Bella gave a whimper of anguish as she reached the same line.

I was due to meet Olivier for lunch in Paris on the day he was shot. In the whole of our relationship I had never known him to be late…

Ashley put out her hand. Bella flinched as it touched her hair, and looked up at Ashley with dead eyes.

'So that's it. He was on his way to meet her. In Paris.' Her gaze moved slowly over the bed, where the scraps of iridescent silk lay like drifts of exotic blossom. 'All this was for her.' She slid stiffly from beneath the covers and shrank back from the bed as if it would contaminate her. 'It's her he loves. Not me.'

Ashley opened her mouth to argue, but closed it again. She had been wrong to give Bella false hope before. The writing wasn't just on the wall—it was in a feature-length article in a national newspaper. All she could do now was deal with the fallout.

CHAPTER SIXTEEN

WHILST the inside of the parish church of St Saviour in the rural heart of Miles's constituency was bathed in beautiful flickering candlelight, the outside was exposed to the full glare of the media spotlight. The marriage of a political figure would usually command a fairly modest level of press interest, but, thanks to recent events, Miles Lawrence's wedding was on a par with that of any minor royal or premiership footballer.

Ashley had played a masterful PR game. From the moment she had emerged with a white-faced and silent Bella from the Paris hotel on the morning the story broke she had faced the press with gratifying openness and brought a touch of vulnerability and humanity to the Delacroix-Lawrence camp. She expressed the family's sincere regret for Olivier Moreau's injury, and said that she hoped that the death of Philippe Delacroix, who it was now believed had been suffering from mental health problems for some time, would mark an end to the long-standing disagreement between the two families.

By the following day the photograph of *La Dame de la Croix,* originally only carried by Veronique Lemercier's article, had been picked up by all the newspapers, and Genevieve Delacroix was an instant celebrity. Her continued elusive silence fanned the flames of media interest to a white-hot firestorm, which was further nourished by Ashley's very discreet drip-feed of information about the picture and the passionate, tragic, *Romeo and Juliet* story behind it. The transformation of the Lawrences in the eyes of the world from dry pillars of the establishment to glamorous, intriguing Euro-aristocrats was swift and complete.

There was an explosion of flashbulbs as the vintage Rolls Royce carrying the bride and her father pulled into the gates of the church and Ashley emerged.

Bella watched her turn briefly to the cameras—enough time for them to get a chance of a good shot but not long enough for it to look tacky—before taking her father's arm and walking towards where Bella stood, shivering in her black silk bridesmaid's dress near the church door.

She smiled. 'You look so beautiful, Ashley.'

It was true. In the dull November afternoon Ashley was radiant. The black and white theme of the wedding, initially inspired by the elegant chequered flooring of the ancient church, provided the perfect foil for the rich colours of the Delacroix cross, which gleamed at her throat.

'Thanks, honey.' Taking care not to damage either of their bouquets, Ashley gave her an awkward squeeze. 'So do you.'

As Bella disentangled herself from the froth of Ashley's veil she gave a bleak laugh. She looked like a train wreck, and they both knew that, although the team of professionals Ashley had hired for the day had brought about some improvement. They had at least put colour in her hollow cheeks and added some sparkle—albeit artificial—to eyes that were dull and lustreless. But they were make-up artists, not miracle workers.

'As it's your wedding day I'll refrain from calling you a big fat liar,' Bella said ruefully, 'but just watch that your pants don't burst into flame.'

Ashley caught her hand. 'You're doing fine, sweetie,' she said fiercely. 'And I wouldn't care if you'd turned up with your head shaved and a tattoo saying "anarchy rules" across your shoulders. I'm just glad you're here. I know that all this—' she waved her heavy bouquet in the direction of the packed church '—was the last thing you needed at the moment, and I appreciate that you're doing it.'

'I'm not sure Miles would take the same view about the tattoo,' Bella said with a weak smile. 'Very bad for his political image.'

'You're far more important to him. You know very well that underneath all that political starch he loves you like mad.'

Bella winced. 'I think we should try and avoid all references to madness in the family, under the circumstances. Come on. Let's get you married off to my overbearing brother, and then we can start on the champagne.'

As the organ launched into the first poignant notes of Pachelbel's *Canon,* Bella took a deep breath and clutched her bouquet of scarlet roses very tightly. The scent of incense and polish mixed with the heady perfume of the flowers as they stepped forward to begin their slow and solemn progress down the candlelit aisle—Ashley on the arm of her father, Bella behind them alone.

Profoundly alone.

Fortunately most of the congregation were too busy looking at the radiant bride and the now-legendary piece of jewellery she wore to notice that the lone bridesmaid, following in her wake like a shadow, had tears spilling down her cheeks.

Walking quickly between the graves behind the church, hidden from the media scrum around the other side, Olivier paused to lean for a moment against a headstone.

With every movement he could feel the bones of his shattered ribs grating together, and even after three weeks the slightest exertion made breathing feel as if he was swallowing fire. When he had discharged himself from the hospital two days ago it had been against the strongest advice of his doctors, but he knew that if he didn't talk to Bella here, today, he might never find her again.

From the moment he had been sufficiently coherent to understand that she had left the hospital, he had ordered Alicia to do everything she could to find her again. Throughout the morphine-drenched days after the shooting a part of his brain had remained perfectly awake, perfectly aware of what had happened and what he'd said, and his physical suffering had paled into insignificance beside his mental torment. He needed to see her so badly.

But the Lawrence ranks had closed round her completely, placing her beyond his reach, and letters and telephone calls to the house in Wilton Square and the shop in Notting Hill had yielded nothing. He'd had no choice but to come and find her himself.

So yesterday, still frighteningly weak, he had gone to the shop, and Celia—visibly shocked by his obvious despair—had eventually relented and passed on the details he needed to get to the wedding. This was his only chance to see her, the only place he knew he could find her, and just the thought that she was so near filled him with fierce determination. Taking a searing breath and ignoring the flare of pain in his chest, he straightened up and carried on towards an arched doorway in the side of the church.

The service was well under way. Music and candlelight enfolded him as he opened the door a crack and slipped through.

He had timed it perfectly. A hymn was just coming to an end. With much shuffling of feet and rustling of service sheets the congregation was sitting down, adjusting cumbersome wedding hats and making themselves comfortable for the reading, meaning that Olivier was able to walk quietly along the back of the church and down a side aisle, unnoticed.

Bella was standing behind the bride and groom, a little to the side. Her head was bent, and candlelight shone on her hair and gleamed from her bare shoulders. In the midst of the quiet jubilation of the wedding service her face wore an expression of unbearable sorrow.

Olivier stopped, leaning against a pillar for support. The

sudden tightening of his chest had nothing to do with cracked ribs or punctured lungs, and everything to do with the girl standing a few feet away in the black dress.

The girl with the trembling mouth and the tear falling slowly down her face.

The girl who at that moment slowly lifted her head and looked straight at him.

'*Love is patient, love is kind…*' the vicar read in solemn tones from the pulpit.

Helplessly, impaled on spears of silent torment, they looked at each other across the candlelit space, separated by a hundred yards of chilly marble and a continent of misery and incomprehension. Olivier's fists were clenched with the superhuman effort of not striding to the front of the church and snatching her into his arms and holding her and kissing her until the shadows had left her face.

'*Love bears all things, believes all things…*'

Bella's eyes flickered closed for a second, as if she'd been hurt. Olivier had to look away then, tipping his head back against the cool stone of the pillar as the words fell between them, taunting and cruel. Gazing up into the majestic sweep of the arched ceiling high above, Olivier Moreau knew that everything he had ever believed in or wanted in his life before this point was nothing.

Money. Respect. Revenge…

Nothing.

The reading ended. There was a pause as the vicar came down the steps from the pulpit, and a murmur of conversation broke out amongst the congregation as the wedding party gathered themselves to go and sign the register. As if from a great distance Bella saw Ashley glance round at her, checking that she was all right, indicating for her to follow them. They were walking across the front of the church towards the vestry.

Towards Olivier.

Bella kept her eyes downcast as they got closer to him. She had gone back to that safe place of numb unreality, removed from the tornado of emotions that raged inside her and battered against the invisible walls of her hiding place. She couldn't think, couldn't comprehend... Couldn't allow herself to hope.

He was leaning back against the pillar. It was useless trying to stop herself looking at him, as pointless as trying to stop herself from loving him. Her mouth went dry and her heart cracked wide open as she saw that his still, impassive face was lined with suffering.

He levered himself up as the bride and groom passed. Bella saw Miles's head whip round, but Ashley steered him into the vestry with steely determination, saying something very quietly into his ear and leaving nothing between Bella and Olivier.

Her footsteps slowed. Neither of them spoke for a moment as their eyes devoured each other, then stiffly he motioned for her to follow Miles and Ashley into the small, cluttered vestry. But while the rest of the wedding group arranged themselves around the registry table, Bella and Olivier stayed separate, instinctively drifting into the shadows at the far end of the room.

He made no attempt to touch her. Part of her was glad—the defences she had built around herself were as fine as spun glass and one brush of his fingertip would shatter them completely. But her own hands shook with longing to reach out to him. Instead she stroked her fingers over the blood-red petals of her roses and looked down.

'You have a habit of appearing when I least expect it,' she said quietly.

'And you have a habit of *disappearing* when I least expect it.'

Bella took a sharp breath in. The coldness of his tone, the cruelty of his words made her want to retreat into the safe place again, away from the welling hurt. She frowned, keeping her eyes fixed on the furled blood-red hearts of her flowers. 'I don't think I can handle any word games right now, Olivier.'

Or any reminders of what happened between us. 'What did you come for?'

He thrust his hands into his pockets and gave a small shrug, as if he was at a loss to know where to begin to answer. 'To say thank you,' he said abruptly, and then gave a short, bitter laugh. 'Some of your perfect manners must have rubbed off on me a little.'

At the other end of the room Ashley and Miles smiled serenely into each other's eyes and there was a flash of white light. The perfection of the tableau they presented provided a cruel contrast with the desolate wasteland that lay between Bella and Olivier. 'Thank you? Thank you for what?'

His voice was like tautly stretched wire. 'For saving my life.'

Unconsciously, her fingers had tightened around a rose petal and she felt it break off, fleshy and fragrant. Instantly she was back in that empty room with her hand on Olivier's heart, his bleeding heart, as the darkness closed around them.

'I just did what you told me to do,' she said hollowly, looking down at the vivid splash of red in her hand. 'You were in control even then. I would have been useless if you hadn't told me what to do.'

'You did it. That's what matters.'

She shook her head, managing a broken, painful smile. 'It was the least I could do under the circumstances. After all, it was my psychotic relative who nearly killed you, and it was me who told him about the painting, so it was pretty much my fault.'

'No, it wasn't. It was *my* fault,' he said through gritted teeth. 'What happened...was no more than I deserved.'

Finally Bella raised her eyes to his then. His expression was devoid of emotion, and in that moment she almost hated him for the pain he had deliberately, ruthlessly caused her. 'Actually, yes,' she said slowly. 'Yes, you're right, you did deserve it, and I can't pretend that if the gun had been in my hand at that moment I wouldn't have done the same thing. You *used* me, Olivier!'

The last words came out on a low note of anguish. His head went back an inch, and he looked more distant than ever. 'Yes. Yes, that's how it started. You were a Delacroix, and I wanted to hurt you—all of you. I wanted to make you feel as worthless as I'd felt, and I wanted the world to know what you'd done. I deliberately seduced you.' He rubbed a hand suddenly over his face, hiding the emotion that flared there for a second, and gave a bleak laugh. 'But I certainly ended up being punished for it.'

'Yes,' said Bella savagely. 'I'd say that a bullet in the chest just about levels the score.'

He shook his head. 'That wasn't the punishment. That was nothing—an accident, that's all. No, my punishment was falling in love with you,' he said bleakly. 'Falling in love with you and knowing beyond a shadow of a doubt that I'm completely unworthy of you.'

At that moment there was a scraping of chairs and the bride and groom got up from the little table where they had signed their names, ready to go back for the last part of the service. As he left, Miles shot Olivier a brief, suspicious glance, but Ashley ushered him forward, telegraphing Bella a look of silent support behind his back.

She stood, completely motionless. And then, very slowly, she began to move away from him towards the door back into the church, shaking her head as if she was trying to remember something important. There was a frown of deep concentration on her face.

'But you were in love with Veronique...' she said painfully. 'I know you were...'

Instantly Olivier moved in front of her, blocking her path, taking her by the shoulders. His eyes blazed.

'*What?* What makes you think that?'

She forced herself to look up at him, holding herself very stiffly. She was focusing all her effort on blocking out the feel of his hands on her bare shoulders, because if she let herself think about how good it was she would never be able to say this, or be strong enough to face the hurt.

'It was *her* name you were saying in the hospital, Olivier. Not mine. It was *her* you were desperate to see, not me. And then I found out that you were going to meet her in Paris that day… You were on your way to meet her, and you had bought beautiful underwear…'

He gripped her shoulders, shaking her very gently. '*Mon Dieu*… For you!' he moaned. 'The underwear was for *you,* because yours all seems to be black…' He looked down at the bridesmaid's dress which hung from her thin frame. 'Black means unhappy. Unloved. And I *never* want you to feel either of those things again.'

Bella put her hands over her ears to muffle the terrifying, wonderful words, because she knew that if she didn't all sense and reason would be lost. 'But the article!' She was almost shouting, past caring about the wedding service that was continuing without her on the other side of the low door. 'All the time you were collaborating with her on an article to ruin us!'

'That's why I had to meet her that day.' He spoke very slowly and deliberately. His hands moved from her shoulders up to her head, and he was holding her face and forcing her to look up at him as he spoke. 'Bella, I'm sorry. I'm so *sorry.* I was on my way to meet her that day to *stop* the article…' His fingers were twining into her hair as he tilted her head up. 'I had to tell her to pull it because I had no interest in damaging the family that I want to make my own.'

Two tears slid down Bella's cheeks, and from beyond the door there was a triumphant blast of Beethoven as the organ started the recessional.

'What?' she whispered, so softly that it was inaudible. Only the movement of her lips, like a kiss, told him she'd spoken at all.

'I love you,' he said ferociously. 'I want to marry you. *Please.*'

She didn't answer. She couldn't, because her mouth, too close to his to resist any more, had found his, and it was a long, long time before she could say anything again.

When they broke apart her bouquet lay bruised on the floor and all trace of the lipstick so carefully applied by Ashley's make-up artists had completely vanished. But, just as it had been that first night at the Tate, her mouth wore the glow of his touch. She pulled back from him, smiling through the tears.

'Hold on. I think that was a thank you, a sorry *and* a please… all in the space of a few minutes.'

His slow smile made her heart turn over. 'You're a very good influence on me,' he said hoarsely. 'I need you. Without you I'm uncivilised and unfeeling and not very likeable. Say you'll marry me or I'm doomed.'

She looked at him from under her hair. 'That's blackmail…'

He shrugged, flinching slightly he pulled her against his broken ribs, and kissed her hair. 'So what?' he said gruffly. 'It's the way our families have always done it.'

The organist was finishing and the church had emptied when they re-emerged. Beyond the doorway in the frosty afternoon the November darkness was lit up by the glitter of camera flashes and filled with the exuberant peal of bells and the frantic clamour of the press. The church was quiet and still.

They stood together in the middle of the aisle. Bella shivered in the ice-spiked air from the open doorway, and held tightly to the lapels of Olivier's jacket. They looked out into the crush of people, isolated by their raw, selfish need to be alone.

'I should be out there,' Bella murmured. She didn't move.

'You'll freeze,' he growled, kissing the angle of her jaw. 'That dress is completely inadequate for this time of year.' His lips brushed her earlobe, her throat. 'And it's black. I don't ever want to see you in black again.'

His mouth was still on hers as he reached inside his jacket and drew something out, and then in the warm candle glow there was a flash of crimson and emerald as folds of papery silk billowed on the chill air. Bella felt him wrapping the shawl tightly around her trembling shoulders and drawing her into him as the tears rained down her cheeks.

'Where did you find it?' she breathed in awe and love.

'Celia's shop. She wouldn't take my calls, so I had to go and see her to try to find out where you were, and that's when I saw it. It made me think of…'

'Olympia. I know. I bought it that morning when you left for Paris. And then…' For a second the anguish crept back into her eyes. 'And then when I got back here I couldn't bear to keep it, so I let it go.'

He folded her into his arms with infinite tenderness. 'You have it back now.'

Bella rested against him for a second, closing her eyes and listening to the strong, steady beat of his heart. 'And you. I have you…' She pulled away from him. 'Did you really just ask me to marry you in there?'

'Yes, but I notice you haven't answered,' he said soberly. 'Does that mean no?'

Joy flooded her, sudden and exhilarating, and she threw her arms out and twirled around in the candlelit church so the silken tassels of the shawl fluttered and the colours swirled and blurred. 'Are you *kidding*? Like I'm going to pass up an opportunity for all of this! I want roses and candles and…and three hundred guests…and a *fabulous* dress, and of course the Delacroix diamonds…'

Olivier leaned back against a pew, watching her steadily. His dark, delicious eyes gleamed. 'Great. Whatever you want.'

She stopped and came back to stand before him. 'Olivier! I'm joking…'

'That's a shame,' he said dryly, brushing her hair back from her face with a fingertip as his lips twitched into a wicked smile. 'I was starting to quite like the idea. That necklace did look very good on you…'

From beneath her eyelashes Bella gave him a look that made his blood sing. 'OK, we'll keep the necklace, then…' Her voice echoed with love. 'But could we possibly leave out all the guests?'

'Deal,' he said gravely. 'And the dress. Could we leave that out too?'

'Oh, yes,' she sighed, reaching up to kiss him gently. 'Yes, please. It's beginning to sound like my idea of a perfect wedding…'

THE MARRIAGE BARGAIN

Bid for, bargained for, bound forever!

A merciless Spaniard, a British billionaire,
an arrogant businessman and a ruthless tycoon:
these men have one thing in common—they're all
in the bidding for a bride!

There's only one answer to their proposals they'll
accept—and they will do whatever it takes to
claim a willing wife....

**Look for all the exciting stories,
available in June:**

The Millionaire's Chosen Bride #57
by SUSANNE JAMES

His Bid for a Bride #58
by CAROLE MORTIMER

The Spaniard's Marriage Bargain #59
by ABBY GREEN

Ruthless Husband, Convenient Wife #60
by MADELEINE KER

HARLEQUIN *Presents*

NIGHTS *of* PASSION

One night is never enough!

*These guys know what they want
and how they're going to get it!*

PLEASURED BY
THE SECRET MILLIONAIRE
by Natalie Anderson

Rhys Maitland has gone incognito—he's sick of
women wanting him only for his looks and money!
He wants more than one night with passionate
Sienna, but she has her own secrets....

Book #2834

Available June 2009

Catch all these hot stories where sparky romance
and sizzling passion are guaranteed!

HARLEQUIN *Presents*

International Billionaires

Life is a game of power and pleasure.
And these men play to win!

THE ITALIAN COUNT'S DEFIANT BRIDE
by **Catherine George**

Alicia Cross's estranged husband has
reappeared—and is demanding his wedding
night! Francesco da Luca wants his feisty
runaway bride back, especially when
he discovers she's still a virgin....

Book #2830

Available June 2009

Eight volumes in all to collect!

www.eHarlequin.com

HP12830

REQUEST YOUR FREE BOOKS!

2 FREE NOVELS
PLUS 2
FREE GIFTS!

YES! Please send me 2 FREE Harlequin Presents® novels and my 2 FREE gifts (gifts are worth about $10). After receiving them, if I don't wish to receive any more books, I can return the shipping statement marked "cancel". If I don't cancel, I will receive 6 brand-new novels every month and be billed just $4.05 per book in the U.S. or $4.74 per book in Canada, plus 25¢ shipping and handling per book and applicable taxes, if any*. That's a savings of close to 15% off the cover price! I understand that accepting the 2 free books and gifts places me under no obligation to buy anything. I can always return a shipment and cancel at any time. Even if I never buy another book, the two free books and gifts are mine to keep forever.

106 HDN ERRW 306 HDN ERRL

Name	(PLEASE PRINT)	
Address		Apt. #
City	State/Prov.	Zip/Postal Code

Signature (if under 18, a parent or guardian must sign)

Mail to the **Harlequin Reader Service:**
IN U.S.A.: P.O. Box 1867, Buffalo, NY 14240-1867
IN CANADA: P.O. Box 609, Fort Erie, Ontario L2A 5X3

Not valid to current subscribers of Harlequin Presents books.

Want to try two free books from another line?
Call 1-800-873-8635 or visit www.morefreebooks.com.

* Terms and prices subject to change without notice. N.Y. residents add applicable sales tax. Canadian residents will be charged applicable provincial taxes and GST. Offer not valid in Quebec. This offer is limited to one order per household. All orders subject to approval. Credit or debit balances in a customer's account(s) may be offset by any other outstanding balance owed by or to the customer. Please allow 4 to 6 weeks for delivery. Offer available while quantities last.

Your Privacy: Harlequin Books is committed to protecting your privacy. Our Privacy Policy is available online at www.eHarlequin.com or upon request from the Reader Service. From time to time we make our lists of customers available to reputable third parties who may have a product or service of interest to you. If you would prefer we not share your name and address, please check here. ☐

HP08R

The Inside Romance newsletter has a NEW look for the new year!

Same great content, brand-new look!

The Inside Romance newsletter is a FREE quarterly newsletter highlighting our upcoming series releases and promotions!

Click on the Inside Romance link on the front page of **www.eHarlequin.com** or e-mail us at insideromance@harlequin.ca to sign up to receive your FREE newsletter today!

You can also subscribe by writing to us at: HARLEQUIN BOOKS Attention: Customer Service Department P.O. Box 9057, Buffalo, NY 14269-9057

Please allow 4-6 weeks for delivery of the first issue by mail.